Angels
in the morning

by

Sasha Troyan

THE PERMANENT PRESS
SAG HARBOR, NY 11963

Library of Congress Cataloging-in-Publication Data

Troyan, Sasha, 1962-
  Angels in the Morning / by Sasha Troyan.
    p. cm.
  ISBN 1-57962-083-3
  1. Girls--Fiction. 2. France--Fiction. I. Title.

  PS3620.R69A54 2003
  813'.6--dc21

                                                        2002030306

Printed in The United States of America

THE PERMANENT PRESS
4170 Noyac Road
Sag Harbor, NY 11963

For Paola Martelli

Many thanks to my mother for being an inspiration in both senses of the word, my father for his support and belief in me, my sister Cybele for reading so many drafts and providing insightful comments. I would also like to thank Deirdre Day-Macleod, Julie Abbruscato and Andrew Zeller for their astute suggestions, Nicole Bokat for suggesting I send my novel to The Permanent Press. A special thanks to Robert Kempe who has helped in more ways than I can enumerate here. Finally, I would like to thank my husband, Kevin, for always being there for me.

One

"If you don't move, it won't get you," my great-aunt Ethel whispers.

From the cloth flowers of my grandmother's mauve hat, the wasp travels to the handle of my governess's white vinyl bag where it rests an inch away from her fingers, each finger the size of two of mine.

"If only it were a bee," Ethel says. "Bees sting only once, and then they die. But this wasp could sting us all and continue on its merry way."

The wasp circles the chauffeur's ear, brushing a tuft of hair.

"If only it were a bee," Ethel repeats, "then it could sting only one of us."

"Who?" I say. If I could choose, I would have a hard time deciding between my governess Juliet and my great-aunt Ethel.

The wasp travels to the rear of the car. It flies straight onto my sister's hearing aid. My sister, Al, lifts one finger as if to stroke it and we all gasp, but then the wasp flies out.

We continue to sit stiffly, however. We don't quite believe it's gone. We lean back against the cream-colored seats only when Granny starts knitting again. Before, when I was little, I used to sit with Granny in the front, but now that I'm ten I'm too big. It's the same with sleeping: before I could sleep in the same bed as her, but now I have to sleep upstairs with my sister.

All I can see of Granny is her mauve hat reflected in the rearview mirror and one elbow appearing and then disappearing behind the seat. I hear her needles clicking and her bracelets jingling. Sometimes, I see a flash as one of her rings catches the sun. But I don't need to see her to picture her eyes, more green than brown today because of the light, her face covered with wrinkles like a cobweb. Once my sister asked Granny why she had so many scratches on her face and Granny laughed and said it was life.

Ethel is not knitting because it makes her feel ill. She's waving a postcard of the Eiffel Tower in front of her cheeks. Her cheeks are usually pink but today they're bright red. She says it's not a sign of health, not at all, high blood pressure is responsible for her color. She says that if her color is an indicator of anything it is of her imminent decline. Ethel always wears dull colored dresses; gray, beige, or brown. She looks like a tall thin shadow following my grandmother who always wears bright-colored dresses.

"Will, did you notice?" Ethel says, waving her postcard more rapidly. "She's lost a lot of weight this year."

"Yes, she has lost a lot of weight," Granny says. "She's lost too much weight. She's lost at least ten pounds, I should say, perhaps even more. She wouldn't say exactly. Don't you think she's lost too much weight, Juliet?"

"I told her," Ethel says, "when you get to be a certain age, you have to choose your face or your figure, but she said she couldn't force herself to eat when she's not hungry."

"She's been working too hard," Granny says, "playing that piano from morning till night, reading that difficult music. It's a wonder she doesn't need glasses."

"But Mummy likes glasses," I say. "When she was a little girl, she pretended she couldn't see so you would take her to the eye doctor and you did, but she didn't get glasses because the doctor realized she was fibbing."

"I hadn't noticed. I've been concentrating on my own weight," my governess, Juliet, says, looking up from her Agatha Christie. She peers over the rims of her glasses, pressing one finger to the page to mark her place, before looking back down again, the tip of her red nail moving along each line, stopping only to wet the tip of one finger before turning the page or to say, "I know who's done it. I always do." I keep moving closer to the window because her arm is sticking to mine, but she just takes up more space.

We reach my favorite part, just before Fontainbleau, where trees, hundreds and hundreds of years old, form a long green arcade. There are so many leaves I cannot see a single thread of blue, and it's impossible to tell the tips of one tree from another.

I kneel on the seat and stare out the back window and Al copies me, but Aunt Ethel says, "Sit properly. You keep brushing your shoe against my skirt."

I articulate without sound to Al, "Arse hole. Pig."

She opens her mouth wide and laughs, making her hearing aid

squeak.

I lean my head out the window. The light is blinding, so I close my eyes and imagine the canoe I'm going to persuade Granny to buy. I'm going to float down the river. I'll lie flat on the bottom of the canoe and look up at the blue sky. I'll fix up my tree house. I'll go swimming in the pool.

When I sit back, the car seems dark. Juliet and my sister Al are singing, "Alouette, gentille alouette." Juliet has closed her book, and her glasses hang from a yellow string. She has slipped her heels out of her shoes. "Je te plumerai le bec, alouette, alouette, aah." Each time Juliet says, "Aah" I can see her purple tongue.

"Stop singing," I say. "You're completely out of tune."

"No, we're not," Juliet says. "Gabriel, what an awful thing to say to your little sister." I stick a finger into each ear and stare out the window. Juliet always defends Alex. It's because she came when Al was a baby. Juliet says she got me too late.

I count the cars passing our car. I wish my father were driving. My father is a good driver. Luis is the worst driver. He only speeds up going around corners. He honks every few minutes and if you point out a cow or a church he swerves off the road. He perfumes his car.

Since everyone is singing, I begin to sing too. I sing as loudly as I can. I yell. Our singing sounds terrible. Everyone sings with a different accent. My great-aunt and grandmother sing with a South African accent, Juliet with an English accent, Luis with a Spanish accent, and Alex on the same flat note.

Then I see a bottle-green car speed by our car. It's my father and my mother. He's coming to surprise us. I recognize the dark brown felt hat he always wears. He won't let me try it on because it's too delicate. But this hat has a red feather. It's not my father, and it's not my mother either. My father is away on a business trip. Mummy says he's in Brussels. He's supposed to come back tonight, but sometimes he comes early to surprise us. He always brings lots of presents. He often gives us boys' toys, like an electric train or electric cars. It's because he hoped we would be boys. That's why we've got boys' names.

Perhaps my mother and father will be there when we arrive. Perhaps they will be sitting on the yellow and white striped chairs by the swimming pool, the skirt of my mother's white dress blowing up in the wind, her high-pitched laugh drifting across the lawn as she tries to hold her skirt down. "Let it go," my father says. "Let it fly."

"Luis," Granny says, startling me. "Do you think we're going to a funeral?" He replies that no one has died in his family and we all laugh except for Al, who gets upset because I don't feel like repeating what he said.

Al's the best lipreader, but she has to be able to see the person's lips. If the person is eating, has a beard or bad teeth, she can't understand either.

"I don't recognize that church. I don't remember it being so run down. Do you?" Granny turns to look at us. "Are you sure we're going the right way?"

"Yes," I say, looking across a field at a small stone church.

"There's only one way, Mrs. Bodley," Luis says as we continue to drive along the straight road with poplars on either side.

"Are you absolutely sure?" Ethel says.

"It's strange," Granny says, "how a place can be exactly the same and yet look different."

Then Juliet screams, "here comes the turn off." The car swerves across the road and my head hits the door. Juliet—everyone in the back—is thrown against me and I cannot breathe. The car screeches and wobbles from side to side. Gradually the wobbling stops and Luis drives slowly again, but it takes us several minutes to believe that everyone is all right and that we're not going to have an accident.

Juliet is the first to recover. She leans over and picks up her white handbag, which makes a clinking noise. Luis passes Granny her hat, and I feel the side of my head for a bruise.

"That was fun," Al says. "Let's do it again."

We all laugh except for Ethel who says, "Certainly not." She waves her postcard furiously even though it is of no use now, badly crumpled between her fingers.

Al isn't afraid of anything because she's deaf. She can't hear witches coming down corridors, creaks overhead. Every night, even though I'm the oldest, I slip into her bed. Al will swing from the highest branch, pet a snake, stand watching a fire spread across a field.

"Oh dear, oh dear," Ethel says. "Are you sure you're all right, Will? Your heart—"

"I'm fine," Granny says, her head appearing around the seat. "Pull yourself together."

"Yes," I say, "or Juliet will have to slap your cheeks like they do in the movies."

"Don't you be rude, Gabriel," Ethel says, opening her handbag with trembling fingers.

"Mrs. Bodley, are you all right?" Luis says.

"No thanks to you," Granny says.

"I wish you'd be more careful, Luis," Ethel says, staring into the mirror of her powder case and patting her nose. "Are you sure you're all right, Will?"

"I'm fine," Granny says. "Don't worry. I only dropped a stitch or two. But what about the suitcases?"

"They're still there," I say. Every summer Granny and Ethel arrive from South Africa with six pink suitcases and one black vanity case, and every year we're afraid the suitcases will slip off the roof.

"Luis, you should have been more patient," Ethel says. "You should have waited to make sure the path was clear. Men lack patience."

"Yes," Juliet says. "Patience is a virtue seldom found in men."

"Unlike women," Ethel says.

"But some men," Granny says, "are not worth being patient for."

We continue to drive through fields. The wheat parts here and there, hiding rabbits or foxes or hares. I can smell the sun in the air, and every few minutes I lift one leg because it's sticking to the seat, or I move forward to let the breeze cool off my back.

I close my eyes and imagine we have already arrived. I imagine the sign for Malsherbes; a white sign with a black line around it. Malsherbes is in big letters, and beneath those letters are smaller ones in script saying, *Pays du miel et des alouettes.* I imagine the long white road cutting through the green fields, the sharp drop, the twist, the turn followed by another drop leading to the old stone house covered with ivy. I imagine the river flowing from beneath the house. As we pass through the white gate, the caretaker, Mme Daudiet, comes running out.

Inside the house it's just as it was the summer before. It's filled with light. Windows are so clean it looks as if there're none at all. Vases are filled with roses and globe thistles and dahlias, and the sound of the river drifts through the open doors.

It's quiet in the car now. I can't even hear the sound of Granny's clicking needles; only the sound of air rushing through windows and cars passing one by one.

The sound of tires crunching gravel awakens me. Al climbs over Ethel's knees. "Can't you wait a minute? You haven't even put on your shoes," Ethel says. "Look at what you've done!" She licks two fingers, then bends over and rubs her calf. The car stops in front of the house with a lurch. Alex jumps out and Luis swings his door open. He walks around the car to Granny's side. Only Juliet does not move. She continues to read. She has reached the last paragraph. I turn and look out the back window. Mme Daudiet is not here.

"All right." Juliet closes her book and prods me with her elbow. "Get out."

"The door won't open," Alex shouts, twisting the handle of the front door. "It's locked."

"Of course it is," Ethel says, placing her hand over Alex's and trying the handle anyway.

"Look under the mat," Juliet calls, rushing past me.

Al flips over the mat. "It's not here." She looks up at Juliet.

"What are we going to do?" Ethel says, throwing her arms out. "I asked your mother twice if she was sure it was under the mat."

"But where's Mme Daudiet?" I say.

"It really is aggravating," Ethel says, leaning towards Juliet.

"Where's Mme Daudiet?" I pull on Juliet's arm.

"Just a minute," Juliet says, glancing over her shoulder and frowning, shaking off my hand. "You can see I'm talking."

"And it's probably too late to call. She's gone by now," Ethel says.

We move back a few steps. We look up at the stone house. Windows and doors are locked. Shutters are closed and ivy grows across some of the windows. Swallows flutter to the roof and disappear under the eaves. One swallow swoops into a broken attic window.

Granny places her hand on my shoulder. "Maybe they've forgotten to lock one door or window," she says. "It's worth a try. You girls go this way and we'll go that way." She wanders off with Ethel and Juliet following behind her.

Alex and I go from door to door trying each handle, but not one door or window will open. Around one corner of the house, Tiger, the cat who lives with Mme Daudiet, appears. She's much thinner than usual and her hair is matted on one side. I wonder where Mme Daudiet could be. Perhaps she mixed up the day. Mummy often mixes up dates.

When we come back to the front of the house, all the grownups have scattered except for Luis. He's smoking, leaning against his car. He has his back to us and he's taken off his cap. Then the front door opens and a man steps out. His clothes are torn and he's barefooted. One of his eyes is made of glass. He glances at us, then hurries round the side of the house. I wonder if he'll bump into Aunt Ethel or Juliet.

Al and I slip inside the house. The air is cool, the stone floor cold beneath our feet. It's so dark we can just see to our left the doors leading to the kitchen and the dining room, our silhouettes reflected in the dusty mirror in the entrance hall. We're wearing the same red dresses with green stems down the front and white collars shaped like petals. I hold Al's hand.

All the shutters are closed. Even the living room with its high ceiling and fourteen windows is filled with shadows. The sun slivers through cracks, lighting a thread of cobweb or a thin layer of dust covering the furniture and the window sills. The smell of damp wood fills the air as if the wood beams lining the ceiling have begun to rot. Vases stand empty. The grandfather clock is silent. The sailboats painted across its face seem to float through the dust. The staircase leading to our parents' room and the music room is missing two pegs which stand against the bottom step. We each carry one. "In case the tramp has a friend or if he comes back," I say. It doesn't look like he's taken anything. A few crumbs on the coffee table are the only trace of his visit. Al and I decide to keep him a secret.

We leave the pegs at the bottom of the staircase leading to our room. We pull ourselves up the back stairs holding onto a red velvet cord as if we were drowning. In our bedroom, there's the smell of damp wool and mothballs. The mattresses are bare. I listen to the river flowing beneath the house. Long ago the house was a mill. Chickens used to cluck and hop around the rooms. But the wheel was removed, and all that's left of the mill is the name; the house is called, "Le Moulin de Doureux," the "dou" like doux, soft or sweet, and the "reux" like the sound birds utter as they glide to their nests. I place my favorite yellow toy rabbit on top of my bed. Juliet is always trying to persuade me to get rid of it because the material is brown in places and it's so faded she's always having to darn it to stop the sponge from falling out. Al puts her favorite toy monkey whose head is always falling off and her white blanket with the tiny blue flowers on her bed. Usually we jump on the beds, but today the house is too quiet.

I push open the shutters in our bedroom. They bang against the outside wall. Then we wander into Juliet's room where the walls are covered with a green cloth that is coming apart at the seams.

I hear the distant tapping of a windowpane or the rattling of a door. Juliet's voice rises from below: "Gabriel, Al, Gabriel."

I run down the stairs through the living room and to the front door. The grownups stand outside. Juliet's forehead is pressed against one of the window panes. Ethel peers over her shoulder, eyes narrowing, as if to make sure we are not hidden in the shadows.

"Open the door," Juliet shouts.

"It's open," I say and turn the handle. I pull, but the door is stuck. Alex puts her hands around my waist, and we pull together. Juliet kicks the door several times. "Keep the handle turned," she says, but still it won't open. "Move," she says. "Al, stand a few feet away." Luis and Juliet lean against the door. It opens, and they come stumbling in. Juliet almost falls and Luis catches hold of her. She breaks away from him. Al and I laugh but then we stop.

"What were you doing?" Juliet says. "That was very naughty of you. You should have come immediately and told us you had managed to open the door. Gabriel, show Ethel to her room, and you, Al, come and help me."

I mouth to Al, "Shit. Merde. Shit."

"Give those to me," Juliet says to Luis who has carried in two pink suitcases. She lifts the two enormous suitcases, swinging them with her as if they were as weightless as the hem of her dress.

"Please," Luis says. "Let me."

I glance over my shoulder at Granny, but she doesn't see me. She's staring up at the sky. She looks smaller this year. I'm almost as tall as her. I want to ask her about Mme Daudiet but Ethel tells me to come and I follow her. Her beige skirt is all creased and twisted. The front is in the back, and there's a ladder in her left stocking. Through the ladder, I can see pale white skin, blue veins and freckles.

Ethel has the worst room. It's long and narrow and even with the shutters open it's very dark. It used to be nicer before they cut it in two to make a bathroom for my grandmother. Ethel sleeps here to be next to Granny. Granny has the nicest room. The river runs beneath her room. It used to have the wheel.

"Where's Mme Daudiet?" I ask.

"She's away," Ethel says. She opens the closet door and peers inside.

"Where did she go?"

"She's away on holiday," Ethel says, opening one of the chest drawers, then closing it.

"But Mme Daudiet never goes on holiday in June. She's always here."

Ethel leans over the chest of drawers to stare into a small mirror with a thick gold frame. With the tips of her fingers, she rubs in streaks of brown foundation which have dripped down her neck.

"Why don't you open the shutters?" she says without turning from the mirror.

I open the shutters and stare through the glass door. There's a weeping willow, behind it a dark fir tree and even further a lone birch.

"Give me a kiss before you go." She presents her brow, closing her eyes as if not to see me. She smells of peppermint.

I open the door leading to Granny's room. She's sitting on the sofa in the shadows holding her hat by the brim, stroking it absentmindedly as if it were a cat. As her hand passes across the brim, a ray of sun catches the cloth flowers revealing their true colors, and the petals tremble and for a second the flowers look real.

I climb onto the window ledges and open the wood shutters. Through one window, I can see the river surging from the house as if eager to leave behind the dark tunnel; it rushes twisting in and out of banks of tall grass and buttercups.

"How beautiful the river is," Granny says, "and even if I can't hear it anymore, I remember the sound." She places her hat beside her. "And isn't it nice to come back each year and find it exactly the same? Just a few cobwebs and dust this time."

"Yes," I say, and it's true now the shutters are open. The sun turns the red rug crimson. The curtains with their green and yellow water lily pattern are barely rumpled, the matching couch only slightly damp to the touch. In one corner, Granny's four pink suitcases stand. Only the ivy has grown. Delicate shadows of leaves flutter on the ceiling and one wall.

I always unpack Granny's clothes. I like to see and touch each silk dress, to smell the mango and avocado scent from the fruit she hides between her clothes. She has dresses which are every color of the rainbow. This year she has three new dresses; a pleated mauve one trimmed with black; a white one with gold buttons, and a blue-green one the color of the sea.

"May I ask you a question, Granny?"

"Of course," Granny says.

"Where's Mme Daudiet?"

"She's—" Granny starts to say, "Come here." She grabs my hand and squeezes it very tight. "She died. She died six months ago."

"She didn't," I pull my hand away.

"I'm afraid she did."

"Will I never see her again?"

"You will never see her again," she says, "at least not on this earth. Who knows what happens after? Your grandfather said he would come and tickle the bottom of my feet to let me know if there's life after death."

"Did he?"

"Well, I'm still waiting to feel that tickle. When I die I'll come and tickle the bottom of your feet." She leans over and tickles the bottom of my foot. "Now," she says, standing up and holding out her hand. "Will you help me make my bed so I can have my forty winks?"

***

I walk across the gravel courtyard to Mme Daudiet's cottage, just as Luis drives up the white hill. He's going to his hotel in Malsherbes. I peer into one window, remembering how neatly Mme Daudiet used to make her bed, each corner perfectly folded, the blue bedspread pulled so tightly there was not a single wrinkle.

"What are you looking at?" Al pulls on my arm.

"I'm looking in the window," I say. "But I can't see inside because it's all dusty." All I can see is Al's reflection: the outline of her round cheeks and her curly hair. Her hair is curly because Mummy and Juliet rubbed lotion in her hair. I wish they had rubbed some on mine.

"Where's Mme Daudiet?" Al asks.

"It's a secret," I say.

"I have a secret too," she says.

"You do not," I say.

"I do too," she says.

"Then tell me," I say.

"I-no-I always go first. It's your turn," she says.

"Mme Daudiet is dead," I say.

"She is?"

"Now what's your secret?" I ask.

"Juliet owns a wig," she says.

"Oh, I knew that," I say. "Let's go see our tree houses."

We run across the lawn, which is knee high, past pink and yellow pansies that stream from broken clay dishes, huge spider like poppies, banks of dahlias and roses. I pretend not to hear Juliet calling from the house. We're barefooted and every few steps one of us treads on a thistle and stops and hops around, holding one foot in the air, shouting "ow, ow," while the other one laughs. We run across a small wooden bridge through tall grass across another bridge and along a bank lined with silver willows and snowballs and a row of red roses. We stop by our trees. Dark ivy covers my tree. One single beam slips through the leaves. Daddy says that one day they might have to cut my tree down because all the branches and even the trunk are rotting, but that will not happen for a long time. For now, it's the best kind of treehouse. Al's tree is healthier than mine, but she wishes she could have mine. Often she helps me instead of working on her own. Our trees are connected to one another. We can climb over a branch and visit without having to touch the ground. We play for a long time.

We swim in the dirty pool. We play our favorite game: banging bottoms. Facing one another, we hold each other's hands, then quickly, as we drop down into the water, we place our feet flat against each other's feet. We pull hard on each other's hands and bang bottoms, our legs going up in the air. We do it over and over again. We laugh, then float onto our backs and stare up at the sky. We leave a trail of water across the white parquet and up the stairs.

***

Standing on the wood bridge, outside Granny's room, I don't need to peer between the curtains to see if she's still sleeping. I can hear her snoring. She doesn't snore evenly the way I pretend to snore if Juliet peeks into my room. Granny snorts. The first time I heard her snore was when I was sleeping in Granny's bed and fell asleep after her instead of before.

I tiptoe into Granny's room. The smell of roses drifts through the open window. The sound of the river is very loud. It's almost like being on a ship. On top of Granny's head Tiger, the marmalade cat, lies. She always settles there while Granny sleeps. It makes me laugh because Granny does not like cats. After lifting the cat off her head, I place one hand flat against Granny's arm, just above her elbow. Her skin is smooth and soft and slightly damp. It reminds me of the cooked white of an egg. "It's time," I whisper into her ear.

"Is it really, dear?" Granny asks. "I feel as if I just laid down." She throws the sheet back and swings her legs over the side of the bed.

Every evening we climb up the hill. Granny won't let Ethel come. I'm the only one. I think she gets weary of Ethel following her all the time. Ethel lives with Granny because Granny is very rich. She's a millionaire. Ethel is poor, but she has better health than Granny. Slowly, we climb up the hill, through an arcade of trees, up stone steps covered with moss. Granny keeps her eyes fixed on the ground and each time we come across a dandelion or a poppy she carefully steps around it.

She pulls on my arm. She bends over and tips the head of a wild yellow flower towards her. She peers inside and inhales deeply and when she looks up her nose is covered with pollen. The gold particles catch the sun. We pass by purple, pink, and yellow dahlias. I pretend not to see Al following us, hiding behind one tree after another.

As we approach the top of the hill, Granny begins to whistle. She whistles so well that if you didn't see her you might think she

16

was a bird whistling behind a bush. She taught me how to whistle and in the beginning when I couldn't whistle very well she showed me how to whistle using a leaf.

At the top, Granny lets go of my arm. She flops down on the grass, slides up her dress and unhooks her stockings from her garters, and slips them off. They float a few feet away like two small ghosts. She slides one hand down the front of her dress and pulls out her cigarettes and then with the other hand she pulls a silver lighter from her pocket. She lights a cigarette. She breathes in deeply and leans back on one hand.

"I suppose the gardener's left," she says. "It doesn't look as if anyone has been here for months." Still there are sweet peas. Their delicate mauve flowers flutter with the slightest breeze, and there are small green tomatoes brushed with pink and farther along, tiny pale green and white strawberries. Overhanging us are laburnums. They line one side of the garden; their gold powder dusts the grass beneath them. Al has climbed to the top of the tallest tree. She has wrapped her legs around the trunk and she is swaying back and forth in the wind.

On the other side of the garden patch, above us, cherry trees grow. Their petals lie in circles like pale pink petticoats abandoned in the heat. Birds swoop from the cherry trees to the mulberry trees, back and forth, their cries filling the air.

Granny's not supposed to smoke. She always tells me not to start. She says it's a filthy habit, but she's too old to stop. Life isn't worth living if she can't smoke, she says. Her father smoked two packs a day until he died at the age of ninety-five. Sometimes Ethel asks Granny whether she has been smoking, and Granny always replies, "What do you care?" Ethel always says, pursing her lips and lowering her eyes, "Oh Will, you know why. How can you? Shame."

"You look just like your mother sitting there," Granny says. "She used to sit like that with her head slightly to one side as if she were listening for something."

"Do I? Do I look like Mummy? Ethel says I look just like Daddy."

"You don't look a bit like him. You've got the Bodley features."

"But I've got big feet and hands." I stick out my hands and Granny puts out her cigarette and takes my hands in hers. Her hands are soft and creamy. Ethel says small feet and hands are a sign of aristocracy. Ethel and Granny have the smallest feet and hands.

"Your eyes—your eyes—are just like mine, almond shaped," Granny says. I stare into her eyes. They are dark green with only a tiny bit of brown.

Ethel's not the only one who says I look like my father. He says I look like him too. His nose was just like mine until one morning he woke up and found it hooked. He says it will happen to me one day. Every night I pray it won't happen, and every morning the first thing I do is run to the mirror and check.

"You'll see," Granny says, letting go of my hands to light another cigarette. "You'll grow into a lovely young woman, and then the two of us will go around the world. We'll travel on the QEII."

I picture us on board the Queen Elizabeth the Second. We're wrapped in blankets lying on chaise longues and drinking consommé.

"Shall we go now?" she asks, putting out her cigarette. She scoops out some earth with one hand, then pats the earth with the other until the stub is hidden completely. She slips on her stockings and her shoes and then I take both her hands and pull her to her feet.

We stand at the top of the hill staring down at the lawn. It dips, levels out, then drops again until it reaches the river. Across the river is the bank of silver willows with our tree houses and beyond it the wild field. The river meanders through the garden, cutting it into islands connected only by narrow wood bridges. The rectangular swimming pool, once turquoise but now green, stands in the middle of the lawn. A stone patio overgrown with moss and black-eyed Susans separates the lawn from the house. The wind blows the grass this way and that way as if it cannot make up its mind.

"We'll see the roses tomorrow," Granny says. "It's almost time for my gin and tonic, and I'm too tired to go any further."

When I glance back at the tree, Alex is no longer there.

"Look who's here," Granny says, looking over her shoulder as she passes into the living room. "Hello, darling."

"Close the door," Mummy shouts as she reaches for pieces of paper floating off the coffee table.

"Mummy, Mummy," I shout, running past Granny.

Mummy turns and clasps me in her arms. "You'd think I hadn't

18

seen you for a week." She holds me away from her and stares at me. Her eyes gleam with tears. "You look so pretty tonight. And how are you?" She turns to Granny and hugs her. "You can't imagine the traffic." Her hands flutter to the back of her head. Her bun is always coming undone. "Just getting out of Paris took me forty-five minutes. I was hoping to get here before you and when I finally did arrive, the house, except for Juliet, was empty. Ethel has gone to the farm. I don't know where Al is."

"She was up in a tree," I say.

"You do look a little frazzled, darling," Granny says. "You've even done your shirt up wrong."

"Oh dear, have I?" Mummy says, looking down at her dress. "I'm always doing that, and I'm covered in dog hairs. I do hope Max hasn't gone off to kill more of the neighbors' chickens."

The first time we came here Max went straight to the farm and killed a dozen chickens.

"Perhaps he'll meet up with Ethel and she'll be in time to stop him," I say. Mummy opens her handbag and fumbles inside, then empties it on the coffee table. We stare at the tortoise-shell comb with missing teeth, a crumpled handkerchief, and a string of pearls entangled in scraps of paper. "Oh dear," she says, "I can't find it."

"What?" I say.

"The key," Mummy says.

"Mummy," I say and pull on her arm. "Mme Daudiet."

"Yes, dear, I know," Mummy says, shoving everything back into her bag. "I wasn't going to tell you right away because I know how fond you were of her."

"What did she die of?" I say.

"She had a heart attack." Mummy avoids looking in my eyes as she puts her hair up and pushes the comb into place.

"Gabriel," Granny says, "will you do me a favor and run and prepare me a gin and tonic?"

"But it's too early," I say, "It's not seven o'clock." Ethel and Granny have a rule about not drinking before seven.

"Please," Mummy says.

I walk slowly to the kitchen. I know they wanted to get rid of me, but I wish Mummy would tell me the truth. I'm not a baby. I stop and stare at myself in the entrance hall mirror. I can't tell whether I look more like Mummy or Daddy. I push my fringe away

19

from my forehead. It's not unusually high like my mother's, but my hair is the same color as hers, brown with reddish flecks and very long. It reaches my waist. Granny used to have hair which she could sit on but one day she had it bobbed, and her father was so furious he would not speak to her for one whole year. Granny says my skin's like hers. My nose isn't like Mummy's either; hers is narrow and ends in a sharp point; mine is broad.

Juliet stands at the sink. She's washing lettuce. She inspects one leaf at a time. She brings each leaf almost to her nose. "I wasn't hired to be a cook you know," she says, without turning around.

I take out the gin and the tonic and prepare Granny's drink, then Juliet turns and says, "Oh it's you!"

"Yes," I say, "I'm making a drink for Granny."

I walk back slowly, my eyes fixed on the rim of the glass. Every time I walk faster it spills onto the stone floor. When I walk back into the living room, Granny and Mummy are sitting side by side on the blue couch. Granny is holding one of Mummy's hands and stroking it.

"Did Granny tell you?" I ask.

"What?" Mummy says.

"We almost had an accident. Juliet screamed 'Here comes the turn off' and then Luis swerved across the road and we almost hit a car and then we almost went into a telephone pole and then Ethel became hysterical."

"I heard that," Ethel calls from the entrance, walking into the living room with a basket filled with eggs. "You're exaggerating as usual, Gabriel."

"She probably gets that from me," Mummy says. "Where's Alex? Isn't she with you?"

"She's playing with the gravel," Ethel says.

"Is Daddy coming soon?" I say.

"Yes," Mummy says, letting Granny's hand drop. "Hopefully, in time for dinner."

"Come here," Granny says, and then she whispers in my ear. "Why don't you run and cut some flowers for your mother's room?"

"All right," I say.

***

We're sitting in the living room waiting for Daddy. The room is

20

filled with shadows, and the face of the girl in the painting which hangs above the fireplace is hidden. I try to remember whether her eyes are green or brown. Sometimes, we have a fire, even in the summer because the nights are cool, but tonight we don't because there's no chopped wood. Juliet's shadow flickers as she leans towards the yellow lamp. She's darning one of my socks. She gets very angry because we walk around the house in our socks. She says we want her to spend all day mending. I saw her put three fingers through the hole of one of my blue socks. She looked over her shoulder and then threw my sock into the rubbish bin.

Ethel and Granny are knitting handbags out of beads. The beads catch the last of the light and are reflected onto the floor. Al and I love to help string the beads on the wool. We love to hide the beads in our pockets and our shoes or we use them to make necklaces for our dolls.

Granny and Ethel are sitting opposite each other, and sometimes it seems as if they're imitating one another because their needles go in and out at the same time. They stop only to take a sip from their gin and tonics. I like to watch them knitting because their eyes become dreamy as if they're thinking of Africa. Perhaps they're thinking of elephants slowly ambling through the bush. Perhaps Granny is thinking of the times she used to take the Victoria into town and buy boxes and boxes of pastries instead of shoes. When my father comes, they'll have to stop. He doesn't like talking to them while they're knitting. He doesn't like the sound of needles clicking.

Mummy's pretending to read *The Brothers Karamazov*. I know she's pretending because she has not turned a page.

"Read to us, Mummy," I say. Mummy reads from *The Four March Sisters*. My sister is too little to understand. She sits by Mummy's feet playing with her doll. Mummy is very sensitive. She cries during passages I don't find so sad. We take turns reading. She gets upset because I'm stupid. I mispronounce words. I have never learned how to read English, because we moved from America to France when I was five. I know how to read only French. She tells me how to pronounce a word and the next paragraph when I see the word again I've forgotten how to pronounce it. Sometimes I wish and wish for the word not to come up again, and for a few pages it doesn't, but then, just when I've forgotten all about it, it reappears.

Once when I was very little and she was reading *The Secret Garden* she asked me the name of the character she was reading and I couldn't tell her and she closed the book and looked sad, but I was listening to the sound of her voice. Sometimes the words made no sense. Sometimes it was like a river and I was looking at the picture in the book and wondering whether I could tame a bird or a fox and have him for a friend. I was looking at the boats on the bed and imagining that they were floating off the bedspread and into the air.

After we have read for a while, Al pulls on Mummy's skirt. "Tell me a story," she says. Mummy tells the best stories, and they all have happy endings. She gives the characters in her stories our names. "Once upon a time," she says, "there were two little girls called Al and Gabriel who woke up one night to find that they had gossamer wings." She has to explain what gossamer is to Al. "They flew up through the sky and the stars." Mummy tells the best story, but when we get to the end she says she feels a bit tired.

"Would you mind if I finish off the story tomorrow?" she says.

"Yes," we say, "finish it now."

"Well," she says, "I've got myself into such a spot I can't think of an ending. Perhaps you can help me."

"No," I say, "we want your ending."

"Very well then," she says, "but don't complain if you don't like it. The next morning Gabriel and Alex awaken and discover that they've lost their magical powers. They can no longer fly the way they used to and they'll have to stay on this earth forever."

"Oh no," I say, "that's not fair, that's a dreadful ending."

"We don't want that ending," Alex says, and bursts into tears.

"I'm sorry," Mummy says. "It's only a story, Alex." She picks Al up and places her on her lap and brushes her hair away from her forehead.

"Please make up another one," I say.

"Now, don't be difficult, Gabriel," Mummy says, getting up. We watch her walk up the stairs and soon the sound of her piano fills the living room. It's the slow sad movement of a Mendelssohn Trio.

I sit on the floor with Alex and we play dolls, but I can't really concentrate. I keep listening, but all I hear is the sound of the piano, the sound of clicking needles, and the river rushing beneath the house.

At seven o'clock Daddy's still not here, and Juliet says the roast beef is going to be completely overcooked. She runs to the kitchen to turn off the oven.

At eight o'clock Al has fallen asleep on the floor. Granny says, "I've had enough. Let's eat. Come help me," and I take her arm and we go into the dining room.

We have dinner in silence because everyone is tired and because we're all listening for the sound of tires crunching gravel. I count the cars passing our house. The front lights shine onto the white wall of the dining room. Mummy moves her food from one side of her plate to the other. Granny eats bread. She eats only the crust. She leaves the doughy part by her plate, and I make little balls of it and pop them into my mouth.

The telephone rings while we're changing plates for dessert. Mummy runs to the telephone. We strain to hear, but there's only the sound of the river, of Ethel sipping her wine, and of Granny's foot tapping against one of the table's legs.

When Mummy comes running back into the dining room, she doesn't say anything. She sits down and, without replacing her napkin, begins eating the melted ice cream very fast.

"Was it Daddy?" Alex says.

"Oh no," Mummy says. She puts down her spoon and plays with her napkin, folding it and then unfolding it. "Just a friend."

"Does your friend know when Daddy's coming back?" Al says.

"Of course not, my lamb, how would they know?" Mummy says. "Perhaps he'll come tomorrow."

Two

A low whistle awakens me. I look over at the window, but there's no bird, just a rectangle of gray sky. I move closer to Al who's asleep, her white blanket with the blue flowers pressed to her nose. Even though I know I'm too old to suck my thumb, I take a corner of her blanket and press it to my nose and suck my thumb.

Usually Daddy awakens me. Every morning he listens to music. He listens to the same piece over and over again. He plays it very loudly. Ethel gets very annoyed. She says she doesn't mind getting up early, what distresses her is Daddy's lack of consideration.

But today the house is silent. There's only the sound of Granny opening or shutting a drawer, the floorboards creaking and the river rushing beneath the house. I hear again a low whistle but much shorter, followed by another two.

I climb out of Al's bunk bed, run down the stairs through the living room where the blue velvet curtains are still drawn, our dolls and books scattered across the carpet and the black and white tiled floor. I peer into the entrance.

"Good morning," Granny says. She turns from the mirror where she is fixing the cuffs of her sleeves. She's wearing my favorite dress of hers, a mauve dress with a pleated skirt. "Are you ready?"

"Yes," I say, staring over her shoulder into the mirror at the reflection of the coat rack. My father's blue jacket and his brown felt are not there. I wonder if my father's wearing his brown felt hat now. I like to watch him put it on. First, he positions it to one side, then to the other and then, when it's exactly right, he smiles. Granny says he wears it to hide his bald spot.

"Shall we go then?" she says. "It's still early, just five, but this way we'll have plenty of time before the sun rises. Aren't you going to wear shoes?"

"No," I say, looking down at my bare feet. "But—I'm not ready. Can you wait for me?"

"Very well," she says, picking up her flower basket, "But don't make me wait too long. I'll be out front."

I run up the stairs to my parents' room. Through the half open door, I can see one corner of their bed and the vase I filled with red roses yesterday. I think I can smell Daddy's cigarettes.

Slowly, I open the door, revealing more of the bed, of the unwrinkled cover, the smooth pillows. The room is so still that at first I think I'm alone.

Mummy's sitting in a chair, leaning forward with her elbows resting on her knees and her chin on her folded hands. She's staring out the window at the white road going up the hill. She's wearing the same shirt and khaki skirt as yesterday. Max is snoring by her feet. I tiptoe across the thick gold rug past piles of unfolded clothes.

"Mummy," I say, placing one hand on her shoulder.

"Ooh," she says, glancing over her shoulder and placing one hand over mine. "You startled me." With the back of the other hand she wipes her eyes quickly and then leans over and runs her hand along Max's short dark brown hair, "You didn't startle him. How did you sleep, my lamb? I'm completely exhausted. I've been dusting and cleaning and then I pulled everything out of the cupboards. I decided it was time to get rid of all these clothes I never wear. They're too big for me now, anyway."

"Could I have them?" I say.

"Whatever for, darling? They would be much too big for you and by the time you're old enough to wear them I promise I'll buy you some that are much nicer than these. I could kill myself for emptying all of the cupboards. Why couldn't I start with one? I was going to ask you to help me, but I think I'd better lie down and rest. The place looks worse."

"It doesn't look that bad," I say. "But you've got cobwebs in your hair, Mummy." I brush them away.

"I'm not surprised. It's just as well he's not here."

"When's Daddy coming?" I say.

"I don't know," Mummy says.

"Is he coming in the morning or the afternoon?"

"I don't know darling, really, I don't. Aren't you going for your usual walk with Granny? Isn't she waiting for you? "Atchew Atchew." I've got dreadful hayfever. Would you mind taking those flowers on your way down?"

"But I put them there for you. Don't you like them?"

"Of course I do. They're lovely. They're my favorite color. I'm so sorry, darling. What a dreadful mother you have! Always saying the wrong thing. I thought it might be the roses making my eyes water. Leave them. Now that they're not right by my bed, I should be all right. I'll see you later, my little friend."

Mummy always calls me her little friend because I'm the only one she can talk to. My sister is too little to understand. My mother says I'm more mature than she was at twenty.

* * *

Roses come into sight one by one as we walk along the white fence. Every few steps I stop to untangle the wet hem of my nightdress and Granny rushes on. I like walking barefooted, feeling the wet grass and earth between my toes. Granny's also walking barefooted. She left her shoes by the road. She takes only three or four quick steps before she stops, and I catch up with her and whisper the name of the rosebush in her ear. Each rosebush has a story, like a person, and Granny tells me how this one was married to this rose, how this other one broke off her engagement with this one, and where each rose is from. Usually I listen to every word she says. I want to remember everything for the next morning so that I can impress her with my memory, but today I want only to ask her where my father is even though I know that as soon as I ask, her hand will tighten on the basket she carries and she will frown, her wrinkles gathering round her lips.

Sometimes, if I linger too long to stare at drops of dew gliding down a stem or hanging from a petal, when I wait and wait for a drop of dew to detach itself from its petal, Granny disappears completely into the mist and all I can hear are her bracelets jingling and the sound of scissors clicking. Sometimes, we catch petals falling from a rose spotting the grass with pink, white, or red.

We don't talk. Granny's listening for larks. They seem to be following us. I listen for them too, but over their songs I hope to hear the sound of my father's car. His car makes a different noise from anyone's. I would recognize it anywhere. Sometimes, I hear a fluttering of wings, but when I turn there is only the movement of a branch swinging back into place. Granny says one rarely sees larks because they're brown and blend in with the thickets. They're not very good-looking birds; it's their flight and their song which is worth waiting for. We pass the Clair Matin, Danse du Feu, Danse

26

des Sylphes, and the ones I always forget the name of, Ghislaine de Feligonde. There are more roses this year than ever before; only the white fence with its peeling paint has suffered from the gardener's absence. Granny cuts one or two roses from each rosebush. She cuts the stems as long as she can.

Once when I was very little and did not know about flowers, I cut off the heads of all the roses along the fence. I placed them in the skirt of my dress and then I ran to my mother and said, "Close your eyes. I have a surprise for you," and when she opened her eyes, I let go of my skirt and the roses came tumbling down onto the floor and Mummy burst into tears.

Granny told me she, herself, was very naughty, even naughtier than I. She used to take her sisters' dolls and bury them in the garden. She would hang by her legs from the branch of a tree and refuse to come down until her sisters had promised to give her their pocket money. She was very fat, so fat she said she could hardly walk through the doorway. Then she went on a diet and she became very beautiful and all the boys went running after her, and she had to pass some on to Ethel who wasn't so pretty. Granny was very lazy. She used to lie in bed eating pastries instead of going to school.

My father says the only reason I'm not first in my class is because I'm lazy, but I think I'm stupid. He doesn't understand because he used to be first in his class. My best friend Catherine is also a very poor student, and we both copy off each other's tests and as we're always both wrong they can't tell whose is whose.

"Let's hurry," I say, pulling on Granny's arm.

"Whatever for?" Granny asks. "I'm too old to hurry."

"Perhaps Daddy's here." I look over my shoulder. The mist has shifted, revealing the lower part of the willow tree, but concealing its middle so that now it appears to be cut in two, the top part unrelated to the bottom.

"Perhaps," she says, "but it won't hurt him to wait for a minute while you walk back with me."

We don't return along the white fence. We walk through the orchard, along the river, which appears and then disappears beneath clouds of mist. And then I see, floating down the river, in and out of bands of mist, my father's brown felt hat. It swirls round and round, not once does it get caught in the reeds.

"Look, look!" I let go of Granny's arm and run across the grass.

"What?" Granny says. "Stop hurrying me. I'm getting all out of breath. What did you see?"

"Nothing," I say. I must have imagined seeing my father's hat. How could it be floating down the river?

The mist turns pink, and the sun's first rays streak the lawn gold. At last we reach the house and step into the kitchen where we leave the roses to soak in the kitchen sink. Granny is going to lie on her bed, and I'm supposed to go upstairs and climb into mine, but I don't.

Instead, I tiptoe out of the house, across the gravel, past my mother's gray car. The sharp stones cut into the soles of my feet. I push open the heavy wooden door and step into the garage.

There's a space where my father's car usually stands.

Perhaps once, when there were haystacks and the door was left open, the barn was a sunny, cheerful place, but now it's cold and dark. In one window, a piece of cardboard replaces a glass pane. Another window is streaked with mud. I shiver and cross my arms. I turn to leave but hear a rustle, coming from the other side of the garage where tools are kept. Perhaps Tiger has hidden her litter in one of the cardboard boxes. I tiptoe across to the other side. Nothing appears to have changed, neither the uneven dirt floor, nor the worktable covered in dust. One soiled yellow glove hangs from a nail; a rake and shovel stand against one wall. Only a piece of brown paper tucked beneath a cardboard box flutters, as if something had just brushed against it, but perhaps it's only the draft slipping beneath the door. I listen to the mournful cries of doves. At first it sounds as if they're outside, but then I think I can hear their wings flapping above. I look up at the beams where garlic usually hangs and almost cry out; hanging across the laundry line are the skins of some kind of animal. They're too big to be rats, maybe they're cats, but their fur doesn't look like cat hair. Their eyes glint in the dark—one is going to jump out at me. I rush to the door and turn the handle but it won't open; it's locked. I run to the other side of the garage, through the door, and across the gravel. I run into the house as fast as I can.

***

"Juliet, I saw some rats," I say.

"Rats," Juliet says, standing in her brassiere and underwear. She

28

does not stop pulling on her pantyhose to look up at me.

"Yes, hanging on a clothesline in the garage."

"How very odd. I wonder what they're doing there?" She hops around the room, lifting one knee, then the other. She seems to be dancing to an imaginary tune and each time her heel comes down particles of dust float up into the air and catch the sun. She weaves in and out of piles of books and clothes. She passes open windows. Juliet believes in fresh air. She stops only when her pantyhose are pulled on without a single wrinkle.

"I saw their eyes gleaming in the dark," I say. The image of them comes back to me and I close my eyes.

"How could skinned rats have eyes?" she says. "He must have cut off their heads."

"Who?" I ask.

"The gardener," she says, "Who else could it be? I saw him hanging them up last summer."

"But the gardener's away," I say.

"Well," Juliet says, "he's supposed to be, but I wouldn't be a bit surprised if he were still lurking around. Just last night I thought I saw a face peering into my window."

"But what are they?" I say.

"They're muskrats. They live in water. Come to think of it, I suppose it could have been your father."

"Not Daddy. He would never—"

"Of course he didn't string them up. He left that to the gardener, but he could have shot them. They have to get rid of them. I don't know why you're getting so upset. It's not as if I told you that your father drowned kittens."

"Do they drown kittens?" I say.

"Of course. What did you think they did with the rest after you'd chosen the one you wanted?"

"You're lying, Juliet," I say and burst into tears, remembering the way Mme Daudiet would bring them in a basket, six beautiful kittens from which we could choose only one.

"Very well," she says, "I'm lying. But your father did shoot muskrats last summer."

"He couldn't have this summer," I say. "Because he isn't here. He's in Brussels now." I follow her into the bathroom. "Do you know what Brussels is like?" I say.

29

"No," she says, "I've never been there, but I should think it's awful. They've got dreadful weather. It's always foggy. Non-stop fog. I expect it's worse than London—do you know that I'd almost forgotten but today's the day—"

"The day?" I echo, wondering whether the small bag I saw the gardener drop in to the river one evening was filled with kittens.

"Go look at the calendar," she says. "It's over my bed."

I stare at the calendar tacked over her bed, a picture of Queen Elizabeth waving from her carriage. Al and I used the calendar to mark off the days until vacation. Now Juliet's going to cross off the days until we return to Paris. She says she was hoping to go somewhere more exotic, like South Africa or Sardinia.

"June 20th," I say.

"Yes," she says. "But look at the day of the week."

"Oh yes," I say. Saturday's the day Juliet does her weekly weighing. She doesn't do it more often because otherwise she gets too discouraged. She lets me watch on condition I don't look at the number on the scale.

Juliet steps onto the scale very carefully as if it might break. She peers down at the arrow.

"Can you see?" I say. "Do you want me to look for you?"

"No, no, run and get my glasses."

Even with her glasses on she has trouble reading, or perhaps she doesn't like what she sees. She leans more on her right foot to make herself weigh less. I look down, and she quickly slides her foot over the numbers, but it's too late. "One hundred and sixty pounds," I shout. "One hundred and sixty pounds."

"You naughty girl," she shouts and runs after me. We run out of the bathroom and into her room. We chase one another, stumbling into books and clothes. We run until she gets out of breath and sits down on her red poof. Her shoulders droop as she says, "I don't understand. I've been on this diet for three weeks. All I've eaten are tangerines and I've managed to put on weight."

I don't understand either how Juliet can eat only tangerines and put on weight. Once I heard Ethel say to Mummy, "We both know why Juliet doesn't lose weight. You really should have a word with her."

Leaning over her red poof, Juliet reaches for a small plastic bag lying on the floor. She plays with the puzzle pieces inside. She took the puzzle out of its box because it took up too much room in her suitcase, but now she can't remember what the puzzle is. Al thinks it's of boats and I think it's of trees.

"Oh well," Juliet says, slowly getting up. She walks back into the bathroom and I follow her. She stands in front of the mirror and draws herself to her full height: five feet and two inches. Her bosoms look as if they're about to burst out of their brassiere. She turns sideways and smooths down her stomach.

"Juliet," I ask. "When did you get breasts?"

"At fourteen," she says. "Rather late, but then they just grew and grew."

She passes her hands over her breasts. She's proud of their size: forty-four, cup D. We both stare at her reflection in the mirror. Her nose sticks out like a parrot's beak. Her eyes are small and brown like tiny pebbles. She's very stocky, but she says she bruises very easily.

"Well," Juliet says, "I must say. I don't think I look all that bad for a forty-seven-year-old lady, even if I haven't lost weight. In a few days, perhaps a week, I'll be able to buy a bikini."

"Oh yes, Juliet," I say. I like to imagine what her bikini will be like. Sometimes, I imagine it a pale pink with gold sequins, sometimes orange with silver beads, and sometimes bright red with black polka dots.

"I almost forgot," Juliet says. "Your room is in a terrible mess. You're to clean it up at once."

"But your room's messy too," I say.

"Don't argue," Juliet says. "Anyway, there's a difference. I know exactly where everything is. Now hurry and then you're to come downstairs for breakfast."

***

The smell of bacon and toast fills the living room. Sun streams through the glass panes, but the air is still cool and drifts through the open windows, rippling the blue curtain hems, blowing away the thin layer of dust covering the dark mahogany furniture and stirring the petals of roses standing in vases. The copper jug on the chest of drawers gleams beneath the painting of the ship, and the gray waves surrounding the ship's bow are tinged with gold. Tiger lies curled up in the sun on the window ledge with her paws covering her eyes.

Only a few cobwebs remain in the corners of the room and in the tops of lampshades. Even the painting of the little girl hanging over the mantelpiece is light. I see that her eyes are green.

The kitchen is even brighter than the living room. Yellow counters gleam and copper pans glint, glasses on the white sink glisten and sparkle. Black-eyed Susans peer at us from behind the window, some have slipped through the opening between the ledge. The sun picks up the red squares of Juliet's rag cloth and the gold specks in my sister's hair. "There you are," Juliet says, "just in time." I dance by her through the kitchen and out into the garden, "Tralalala tralala."

"Where are you going?" Juliet shouts. "I've got a treat for you. Come back. Have you ever tried bread toasted in bacon fat?"

"No," I say and sit down. It sounds terrible, but when I try a piece it's delicious and Juliet makes me a second one.

Al's already had two, now she's having a third. She's got egg all around her mouth. Her eyes are still sleepy.

Juliet says I don't have to worry about my weight. I'm skinny, and I'm still growing.

"I'm going to be a dancer when I'm older," I say.

"I think it would be very nice to be a dancer," Juliet says. "I wanted to be a dancer when I was a little girl." I can't imagine Juliet as a little girl flitting across the stage in a white tutu. I can't even believe she was ever a child.

"I know," I say. "And that's why you've got bunions on your feet. From dancing on points at too early an age." Juliet's the one who told us about her bunions.

"Why didn't you wake me?" Al asks.

"Because," I say.

"Because why?"

"Because Granny and I had things to discuss," I say.

"But you promised I could come," she says.

"Besides you have your speech therapy," I say.

"Not that early," she says.

Every morning Al and Mummy do speech therapy. They say the same words over and over again. But sometimes they draw pictures. In Paris, Al has a speech therapist. I think it must be nice to be deaf because then everything you say is interesting.

I jump up from my chair and run outside screaming at the top of my lungs, "Follow me." Al screams too, but then Juliet yells for us to be quiet. She points to my mother's bedroom. I think I see Mummy peering through the window.

We creep up to Granny and Ethel. They're already sitting in the blue foldout chairs on the stone patio. They're knitting. The brims of their hats waver as they slip their needles in and out. They look as if they're talking to one another, but they're not. They whisper, "One plain, one purl, one plain, one purl," and sometimes they shout, "Oh dear, I've dropped one," and you would think they had dropped a real pearl if you did not know about knitting.

"One, two, three," I mouth to Alex and then we shout, "Boo," and Ethel almost falls off her chair.

"You'll give me a heart attack you will, you're impossible. I shall have to talk to Juliet," Ethel says. She looks down and retrieves two or three dropped stitches. "Never mind me. You'll give your grandmother a heart attack. Are you alright, Will?" she shouts.

"I'm fine," Granny says. "I'm getting so deaf I barely heard them. No one can give me a fright anymore. Gabriel, why don't you get a chair and I'll show you how to knit?"

"No thank you," I say. "Maybe later. I've got a lot of work to do on my treehouse."

"You be careful," Ethel says. "Don't climb too high, Al."

We run across the small wooden bridge through tall grass across another bridge and along the bank lined with silver willows and snowballs and red roses. We stop by our trees. I send Al to get logs to make a bunkbed for my tree. I wish my tree were taller than the house so that I could see the white road leading to the gravel court-yard. I hope Daddy comes soon. We always go to the market on Saturdays and the morning is the best time to go. By evening all the good fruit and vegetables are gone. My father knows everybody and before buying anything he tastes it. The vegetable man doesn't mind because my father buys so much. He even lets me try the tomatoes and apricots.

Across the river, I can see Granny and Ethel knitting. Sometimes, Granny's mauve hat blows off. It rolls over and over through the grass and Ethel runs after it, one arm outstretched, one hand holding down her own pink hat. "Stop, stop," she calls.

Later, Juliet sits between them. She does not wear a hat. She leans over one side of her chair and then the other, back and forth between Granny and Ethel. I see her point at Mummy's room.

I think I hear Daddy's car, but each time I'm wrong. At twelve I hear the bakery car honking as it goes over the hill. Juliet leaps up from her chair. We expect her to call us for lunch, but she does not come. We play and play in our trees. We dress our dolls. The small dolls are the good, pretty ones, orphans left in charge of the big nasty dolls. The big nasty dolls punish the small dolls by putting them on a diet of crumbs and a thimble of water. The big dolls whip the small dolls with small swatches of willow. The big dolls put lemon on their wounds.

Then Al grabs the "*Gone with the Wind*" doll from me.

"That's mine," I say. "Daddy gave it to me for my birthday last year."

"No he didn't," she says. "He gave you the one with the blue dress and the pink sash."

She turns away from me so that she doesn't have to hear what I say, and I try to twist her head around so that she'll have to see my lips, but she closes her eyes and Juliet arrives and asks me why I'm torturing my poor little sister. It's not fair. Juliet is always on her side.

I decide not to eat a thing so that they will be sorry, but I'm so hungry that I eat half a baguette with boursin, Granny's favorite cheese. Mummy does not come downstairs, and in the afternoon while we are napping, the sound of her piano drifts up to our room. Daddy does not like Mummy to play. He always says, "Why do you have to play as soon as I come home?" and later, if she continues to play, he says, "Boy, do you attack those keys aggressively." Sometimes, I think she has finished playing and he has come, but after a minute or two, she starts up again.

At four, Juliet says we may get up, and I tiptoe to Granny's room to wake her from her nap to go up to the vegetable garden. I won't let Al come. "Go away," I say. "Don't follow me everywhere." Mummy and Granny's voices drift down into the living room. They're arguing. I can't make out the words because they're talking in whispers and the door to Mummy's room is closed. As I tiptoe up the stairs, Mummy's voice becomes louder, but then Granny starts talking at the same time as her. Granny says, "I do hope—"

"Please," Mummy says. "I know—"

"Get angry.—"

"Please, please, please, can we not talk about it?"

I knock lightly on the door. "Just a minute," Mummy says.

Mummy is sitting in front of her dressing mirror and Granny is standing behind her, slowly brushing Mummy's hair. Her hair is electric and sticks to Granny's arm. I count the strokes, and then I stand beside Mummy. She's twisting round and round the silver top of an empty crystal jar.

"Granny and I are going into Malsherbes," Mummy says.

"Aren't we going to go up to the vegetable garden?" I say, turning to Granny.

"Not this evening, dear," Granny says. "Maybe we'll get you a surprise."

I stroke Max's ears as Mummy and Granny leave the room and Max moans as if he were sad that he too cannot go to Malsherbes.

Then I stand looking out Mummy's window, waiting for Mummy and Granny to come out the front door, letting the white curtain wrap itself around me, wondering whether I look like a ghost. I watch them cross the gravel, Granny stop to lift some flowers which have fallen. I wonder what the surprise will be. I hope they're planning to buy me a canoe to go down the river. I watch them get into the car. They both sit in the back. The car glides up the hill, then disappears over the top.

Everything in Mummy's room has been put away. Even the vase with the red roses. The wind blows, lifting the curtains and swinging one of the closet doors open, revealing hangers without clothes. I listen to the hangers jingle until the wind stops and they hang still. I open the other cupboard door. My father's suits have gone; his ties, the long row of shiny shoes have disappeared. All that's left is a black shoelace stuck to the plastic covering Mummy's favorite cream dress. His sweaters have been replaced with a stack of Mummy's music, and there's no sign of the tiny leather horse my father kept wrapped in a scarf because it was coming apart, the yellow stuffing spilling out at the seams.

I check the other cupboards. They too are bare, but beneath their bed, I find a dark blue suitcase, overflowing with clothes. The suitcase used to stand upstairs in the attic; once, when we were playing hide-and-seek, I hid inside it. I drag the suitcase from beneath the bed and flip it open. A photograph of my parents at their wedding lies on top of my father's clothes. My mother holds white lilies, while my father wears a gray top hat. Monogrammed handkerchiefs, suits, socks, cufflinks, shoes, ties, even the leather horse, have been thrown in; only his brown felt hat is missing. Perhaps I did not imagine it floating down the river this morning.

I hear Juliet calling me and push the suitcase beneath the bed, then run across the soft carpet, but suddenly I feel something enter my foot. Hopping on one foot, I dash to the bathroom. I place my foot in the beam of light slipping between the blinds, twist it from side to side until at last the sun catches a tiny shard of glass.

***

"I don't have all evening," Juliet says. "Luis is coming at seven thirty and I still have to get ready." She bends over and carefully places two bowls of soup beside another bowl on the round white kitchen table. The light in the kitchen is softer now. Max is snoring by my feet. Sometimes, he shudders or moans as if he's having bad dreams.

"Remember your manners, girls," Juliet says. "You may begin. Don't blow on your soup."

"But it's too hot," I say.

"It's too hot," Al repeats.

"Then you must wait until it isn't." She wipes the corners of her lips with the tip of her white napkin. "Gabriel, how many times do I have to tell you to position your spoon correctly? Like this." She grabs my spoon and twists it so that it is parallel to my mouth and not perpendicular. "Don't make that noise. Watch me." She brings the spoon carefully to her mouth and sips her soup. Her purple tongue appears. "See?" she says.

I take a few more sips, making a lot of noise each time. Al sees me slurping and grins at me from across the table.

"You're doing it on purpose," Juliet says.

"No, I'm not," I say.

"Don't argue with me, Gabriel, or you'll be sent to bed without any dinner. Sit up straight. Your manners are terrible, and they seem to become worse and worse. Your hands. Keep them off the table."

"The French think it's rude to keep your hands off the table," I say.

"Perhaps," she says, "But that's the French. Your mother hired an English governess."

"Daddy said the French have that rule because they're afraid people will be holding hands under the table," I say.

"Really?" Juliet says. "Well, I can't say I'm surprised. But your father is American."

"Max farted," I say, and Alex and I giggle.

"How many times have I told you to use the words 'pass wind' if you must refer to such things?"

"Max has passed wind," I say. "And I think I've passed wind too and Alex has too."

Alex giggles very hard.

Juliet hits me behind the head, and my spoon flies through the air, but I don't cry because I don't want Juliet to think I'm a weakling like she says the French were during the Second World War. She says the English were the brave ones. They took hundreds of boats across the channel to save the French.

"I think I got you too late," Juliet says as she replaces our soup bowls with clean plates. "I really have to get children when they're babies, before they can even walk. I suppose I'm not strict enough with you. But really, I think that Americans don't know how to bring up their children. They're too lenient. The English know how to prepare their children for life. Even our English royalty is brought up strictly. Prince Charles used to have to take icy cold showers at boarding school. You really can't expect to make a boy into a man if you molly-coddle him and let him do what he wants and of course, going to the army is essential."

"Daddy never went to the army," I say.

"No, he didn't," she says.

"He says he's going to send us to military school," Al says.

"Well, that might not be a bad idea," Juliet says.

"I'm the horriblest naughtiest little girl in the whole wide world," I say.

"I didn't say that, Gabriel," Juliet says. "You're always exaggerating. You just need to make an effort. You can be little angels when you put your mind to it. Look, I'm going to trust you girls and let you finish your dinner on your own. I've left some apple crumble on the counter."

Juliet used to call us angels in the morning but she hasn't in a long time.

"Where's Brussels?" I ask Juliet who is standing in front of the full-length mirror in our bedroom. She doesn't answer, but leans closer into the mirror, forehead almost touching. She says the mirror in our bedroom is more flattering than the one in the bathroom. Al and I are sitting on the bottom bunk bed. We always watch Juliet getting ready for her evening off.

"Hmm," she says. With her lipstick, she carefully draws a red circle to match the one on her other cheek. She does not rub the circles in immediately so that for a moment she looks like a clown. All she needs is a little red circle on the tip of her nose. "Brussels is in Belgium and Belgium, well Belgium is close to France." She leans away from the mirror and pinches the shoulders of her black satin dress, lifting the bodice slightly, only partly concealing the white powder gleaming between her bosoms.

"Where are you going, Juliet?" I ask. She turns sideways and inhales deeply, passes one hand over her stomach and tightens her gold belt by one notch. "Are you going on a secret rendez-vous?" I ask. She bends over and pulls on her stockings and I wonder whether her wig will fall off, but it doesn't. I know she's wearing a wig because her own hair is so thin you can see her scalp shining through.

"Stop, Gabriel. You're like a radio. Talking on and on. Run along and tell Luis I'll only be a minute," she says.

Luis is leaning into his car and spraying it with more perfume. "She's always late," he says, looking over his shoulder.

Juliet says it's good to keep men waiting. When we stay at a hotel and have dinner with her, she always makes the waiter stand for a long time while she tries her wine. "A bit dry but it will do," she says, holding her glass high in the air with her pinky sticking out straight.

By the time I get back, Juliet has smoothed in the red circles and brushed her eyelids with purple and blue powder.

"Are you sure you can't see the petticoat?" she asks, twisting her neck around. She tugs on the skirt of her dress.

"I'm sure," I say.

"Run and get me a tissue," she says.

She puts her tongue to one side of her mouth, then to the other. She wipes the corners of her lips with the tissue. We hear Luis honking several times. "Oh that man," Juliet says. "It will only make me take longer."

"Are you going on a secret rendez-vous?" I say.

"Yes," Alex whispers, eyes widening, "a secret rendez-vous."

"Maybe, maybe not," Juliet says.

"Maybe, maybe not," I say, imitating Juliet's voice.

"Now, Gabriel, don't you be rude," she says.

I hate grownups. They never want to tell you anything.

I mouth to Alex. "Juliet's wearing her wig. I dare you to pull it off. Go on."

"You'll see," Al says.

Al goes up to Juliet and says loudly, standing the way Juliet often does with her hands on her hips, "You're wearing a wig."

"No, I'm not," Juliet says.

"You are," Alex says.

"No, I'm not," Juliet says.

"Yes, you are," Al reaches up and touches the wig.

"Don't you dare touch it or you'll be sorry," Juliet says.

Alex reaches for it again, but Juliet steps back.

"Don't you dare," Juliet says.

Al jumps up and pulls on the wig, but it doesn't come off because Juliet has attached it very carefully with many hairpins. Al leaps up again, and this time the wig falls off and Juliet screams. "I've had enough. I'm leaving. Now." She bangs her door shut.

Al's face flushes as she stands holding the wig. She starts to cry, but I tell her not to worry. Juliet's not going to leave. She's been threatening to since the day she arrived, almost seven years ago, just after Al was born.

But I'm not sure I'm right. We've never done anything this naughty.

Carefully, I take the wig from Al. The hair feels different from real hair, coarse and stiff. I'm not sure what to do with it. In the end, I fold it in two and push it beneath the armchair.

We open the door in our room that leads to the attic. We climb the stairs. We're not allowed in the attic because it doesn't have a proper floor. It only has beams so we have to be careful not to slip or we could fall all the way down to the living room and land on Granny while she's having her gin and tonic.

We stand looking out of one of the attic windows. We can see the swallows from up close now. We take turns holding each other's legs to look at the nests with the little babies. Their orange mouths are stretched wide open, and they cry for more food. We know we must not touch them or their parents will abandon them and they will die. When it's my turn at the window, I see Mummy talking to Luis.

We hear footsteps, light ones, hurrying up the stairs. They're Mummy's. We hear her knocking on Juliet's door. We tiptoe down the stairs from the attic and open the door leading into our room. I hear Mummy say, "I just came up to let you know that Luis is waiting." I lipsing everything to Al.

"Well, he's going to have to wait," Juliet says.

"Is anything the matter?" Mummy says.

"Nothing at all," Juliet says. "I've had enough. I'm leaving."

"Oh no," Mummy says. "Whatever happened?"

"Nothing at all," Juliet says, "Nothing unusual, that is."

"But something must have happened to put you into such a state. Gabriel, Alex," Mummy calls.

We walk slowly down the stairs, into Juliet's room. She does not stop packing.

"What did you do?" Mummy says.

"She pulled off Juliet's wig," I say, "but Juliet lied. She said she didn't have a wig, and I told Al to pull off Juliet's wig."

"I'm so sorry, Juliet," Mummy says and then, turning to us, "You're to apologize immediately."

"They can apologize," Juliet says, "but I'm still leaving."

"Juliet, please. I can't bear it," Mummy says. "You naughty, naughty children. Why do you have to make my life so difficult? Can't you see that it's hard enough for me already? You're to go in your room and wait there until I tell you to come out."

We lie down on our beds and press our ears to the wall, but I can't hear anything because they're whispering.

"Got off lightly, if you ask me," Juliet says after Mummy has gone. "If you're not good, you'll be sent to boarding school and believe me you'll learn manners there."

It's too early to go to sleep. It's still sunny in our room. Daddy and Mummy have already talked of sending me away to boarding school. They say I have no self-discipline. My father says I lack self-confidence. He says to get rid of the problem I must stand in front of the mirror every morning and beat my chest and shout, "I'm great. I'm great."

When I'm feeling sad, I imagine myself floating outside of my body and into the corner of the room. Floating out of my body also helps me to go to sleep. Juliet says the best way to fall asleep is to think of sheep, but it never works for me. I think of the grass and the fence. I see one sheep after the other jumping over the fence, and then I hate the fence and get rid of the fence and then the grass and watch the sheep not jumping, but floating through the air. Later, when the sun has dropped and the air is cool, I climb into Al's bed and she lets me use one corner of her white blanket. Al can't lip read in the dark so we write across each other's palms. We laugh, remembering the time in Paris when we were reading our books under our sheets with flashlights and I attached a string to Al's toe that went from her room to mine so that I could warn her when Juliet was going to come but Juliet tripped on the string and landed with a big thud that woke up Mummy and Daddy who came running upstairs. Then Al and I both have to pee at the same time. We can't be bothered to go downstairs to the bathroom, so we each take turns sticking our bums out the window.

Three

We're walking up and down the stairs, in and out of the light that streams through the window. We're gliding our dolls along the red velvet cord. Our dolls are slaves that have to do everything we tell them. Granny's still asleep. She did not wake me to see the roses. Tiger, the cat, lies across her head. Juliet sleeps sitting up with her head resting against the wall. She's started her puzzle but she's done only a few pieces. Ethel has the covers drawn over her head, while Mummy lies with Max. He's snoring very loudly and passing wind. The grownups were up late last night. The telephone rang several times. I wonder if it was my daddy. We heard footsteps. I thought it was a witch and slipped into Al's bed.

We wander through the house playing you can't touch the floor. We start on the yellow couch, then jump onto the carpet. Carpets don't count as floor. Getting from the carpet to the bannisters is very hard. The white tiled floor is the ocean.

Then Granny appears in the doorway of her room. She says that we're going to go into Malsherbes so that Mummy can get her beauty sleep. We're going to pick up my surprise. The camping store was closed yesterday. I'm sure it's a canoe. Granny says not to wake up Juliet. She had a late night. Al and I skip around the house, singing, "Juliet and Luis. Juliet and Luis." Ethel insists we wear the red dresses with green stems down the front and white petals for collars, black patent shoes and white socks. It looks like we're dressed for a party. I hate wearing the same clothes as Alex. Once I asked Mummy why we had to wear the same dresses and she said because we look sweet.

When we get into the car, I ask Granny and she says that next time she'll send me a different-colored dress. She makes us laugh by pronouncing the names of nearby towns. She pronounces Malsherbes, Mallerbee, and Pithiviers, Pit-iv-ers. She tells Luis she's thinking of walking next time—she'd get there quicker. She lets him swerve across the road like a fish even though Ethel complains.

Since we've left, Ethel has been trying to find the right page in her Michelin book. She just looked up again and said, "These French. Why don't they include an index?"

"It's a typical French day," Granny says. The sun is trying to push through the clouds. Sometimes the clouds part for a minute and we see the sun but then the clouds cover it again.

"I suppose he thinks he's just behaving like a typical Frenchman," Ethel says. "Do you think he'll be—"

"Sh—" Granny says, placing one finger over her lips. "I wouldn't be at all surprised. That's why I thought it best—"

"I've found it at last," Ethel says. "Malsherbes. An unremarkable town. Really, what do they know? I think it's charming."

"Quite charming," Ethel says as we sit in the main square of Malsherbes, under a white parasol. "If only they wouldn't blare that awful music." There are huge speakers attached to many of the buildings.

"I can barely hear it," Granny says.

"Maybe you're getting deaf like Al," I say.

"Maybe I am," she says.

We watch people weave in and out of stalls. Sometimes they stop and stare at us because we're so dressed up compared to them. They probably think we look silly. Most of the older women are dressed in black. Granny and Ethel are dressed in pink and green. There are two markets. This one is for clothes. Large pink, yellow, and white underwear are on display beside spools of wool and reels of cotton, socks and tapes, old nightdresses. "Demandez. Demandez," stall owners shout. Pigeons fly over the blue roofs. One swoops right over us. Through the white canvas, we see its shadow.

We go into a camping store and a man with a gold mustache shows us different kinds of inflatable boats. I have to translate for Granny. I choose a bright orange inflatable canoe. We buy a red pump and an oar and there's even a little square piece of plastic with a tube of glue in case the boat gets a hole. I tell Granny I'm going to call my boat the QEII. She makes Al and me promise not to go beyond the grounds that belong to our house where the river is more like a rapid. If we want to go further, we must bring an adult. We laugh at the thought of Ethel or Juliet accompanying us.

43

As soon as we pass through the white gate, I smell the cut grass.
I see his shiny black briefcase in the entrance hall. I run through the
kitchen, past crates overflowing with fruit and vegetables, past glow-
ing oranges. Their scent mingles with the scent of cut grass and
lingers even as I run outside the kitchen door and across the stone
patio towards the pool where Mummy sits in a yellow and white
striped chair across from Daddy. But as I rush across the grass,
through the cut path, I'm afraid that it won't be him, even though I
can see the shadow of his long legs on the grass and the top of his
head above the chair. I'm afraid until I reach him and he smiles and
jumps up from his chair and swings me up in the air. He swings me
high; he does not care that I'm ten, round and round we go, higher
and higher.

"Somebody's happy to see me," he says, putting me down and
then swinging my sister Al through the air. He swings her faster and
faster. He never gets dizzy. "Guess what I've just bought myself?"
he says, sitting down. He leans back and places his hands beneath
his head.

"A watch," I say. Our father has a collection of watches.
Sometimes I see him lifting them out one by one from a silver box.
First, he wipes the face with his handkerchief, then he brings the
watch to his ear, and if he can't hear it ticking he winds it up.
Sometimes, when he takes a pocket watch out, he swings it by its
gold chain, and I watch the shadow go back and forth across his
desk. He almost never wears a watch, but when he does, he wears it
on his right wrist. He's worn it on that wrist ever since he broke his
left wrist falling from a tree when he was twelve.

"A good guess," he says, "But not the right one."

"A car," Alex says.

"A shirt," I say. Daddy has hundreds of shirts of every color,
and each drawer is labeled for a different color. Sometimes, I open
his closet door and close my eyes and pull out a drawer and guess
the color.

"No, no," he says, "I'll give you a clue." He takes his hands
from beneath his head and leans towards us. He whispers,
"Something which will enable you to see yourselves exactly the way
you are today."

We stare at our father. He isn't wearing his brown felt hat. He's wearing a white shirt and a blue suit the same color as the swallows. His face is tanned, and as he smiles two white lines run from the sides of his nose to the corners of his mouth. It's very quiet, so quiet we can hear the buzzing of wasps and bees.

"It's not written on my forehead," he says and uncrosses his legs, revealing a black box lying in the grass beneath his chair.

"A camera," I say and jump up in the air.

"You cheated," Alex says. She pulls on my arm. "You saw it. That's not fair."

"Now don't you two fight," he says, pulling the camera from beneath the chair and then standing up. "I want to take some photographs. Where shall we go?"

The wind blows, and the cut grass swirls through the air, covering us with tiny bits of grass, flecking Mummy's peach dress and Daddy's white shirt, tickling my legs and the back of my throat. The grass has covered the pool. But I do not want the wind to stop. I look up at the sky and will the wind to keep blowing and the sun to stay, but the clouds close on the sun again, and the grass is blue and I can hear the buzzing of bees and wasps again.

"How about in front of the pink roses? On the stone wall?" Daddy says. We sit on the stone wall, swinging our legs, waiting for Daddy who is kneeling on the grass to adjust his lens. "Get out of my way, Max," he says, as Max, our dog, circles him. The clouds and the sky are reflected in his lens.

"Smile," he says. "Don't move." I stop swinging my legs. I even hold my breath.

"Watch for the birdie," he says. A bird is going to fly out of the black box. Soon I shall see its black wings unfurl from the lens. Click.

Daddy turns and asks Mummy to come, but she says she doesn't feel like having her picture taken. "I look dreadful," she says, leaning against the kitchen door.

"No, you don't," he says. "You look lovely. Doesn't she look lovely?" He turns to us.

"Oh yes," Al and I say. "She looks lovely."

Mummy is wearing a peach colored dress with tiny pearl buttons down the front and the hem makes little ripples like the water in the wind. With one hand she tucks in a strand of hair which has escaped

45

from her bun. She tries to flatten the curls framing her face.

"Leave them," Daddy says. "You look even more lovely with your hair undone and even an unraveling hem." Mummy reaches for her hem and pulls on the white thread, unraveling it even more.

"I think you're fishing for compliments," he says.

"You're fishing for compliments," we shout.

"No, really," Mummy says. "I just don't feel like having my picture taken. Anyway, I always look so dreadful in photographs, all teeth and gums."

"Oh come on," he says. "Don't be a spoilsport."

"Don't be a spoilsport. Don't be a spoilsport," we shout.

She comes and sits between us. She holds my hand. Her hand is smooth like the petal of a rose, but cold.

"Give me a smile," Daddy says. Our father takes many photographs. He stops only when Granny and Great-aunt Ethel come out. They have brushed their hair and applied fresh lipstick. Granny has lipstick on her teeth. When I tell her, she takes out her handkerchief and rubs her front teeth.

Daddy kisses Granny and Ethel and then he says, "Why don't we have some pâté and bread and apple cider? I bought some in Malsherbes—pâté d'alouettes. I'll run and get it. Gabriel and Alex, bring the blue fold-out chairs."

All the grownups sit in a circle by the pool. At first they don't say anything. They concentrate on balancing their plates upon their knees. They spread pâté on thick brown bread. Alex and I lie on our stomachs, our chins resting on our hands. When the clouds part for a second and the sun appears, the silver knives and Daddy's gold cufflinks glint.

"Did you have a pleasant trip?" Granny says. She holds her knife in the air.

"Yes, thanks," Daddy says. "The weather was terrific."

"I can see that by your tan," Granny says. "I trust it was not too fatiguing."

"Oh no," Daddy says, looking up from his plate. "It was quite enjoyable."

"Well, I'm relieved to hear that," Granny says.

"Mother," Mummy says.

"And the food," Granny says, "You must have missed that."

46

"I can't complain," Daddy says, "the food was excellent."

Granny snorts, then purses her lips, "Since everything was so very excellent, I'm surprised you could tear yourself away at all."

"Mother, really. Please," Mummy says. She places one hand over Granny's.

Daddy does not say anything but leans over and tries to brush the grass out of the cuffs of his trousers.

"Come," Alex says, pulling my shoulder.

"Not now," I say, moving away.

"Why?" she says.

"Because," I say. She pulls on my pony tail.

"Stop," I shout. "Stop pulling my hair." I push her away.

"What's going on?" Daddy asks, throwing a handful of cut grass at me.

"She wants to play," I say.

"Why don't you?" Daddy asks. He throws another handful of grass at me.

"Don't," I say.

"Go on," he says.

"All right," I say, slowly getting up from the grass, scowling at Alex. We climb up to the top of the hill and then we roll down. At first I go slowly. But then Alex says, "Let's race."

"All right," I say. I'll show her. We run up and then we roll down, faster and faster. We get all dizzy, but we don't care. We shout and laugh. When we stop, we're all hot and Al's cheeks are very red and her dress has green streaks down the front. We have cut grass in our hair and down our dresses and in our pants.

We lie on our backs and stare up at the sky. More and more clouds are gathering. Swallows swoop lower and lower. They pass close to one another, but never brush each other's wings. We turn on our stomachs and stare at the grownups. All we can see from here are their feet and their legs: Granny's wearing white stockings and tiny purple shoes, her feet barely touch the grass; Mummy's legs are hidden by her dress; Ethel has placed both her feet side by side; and Daddy keeps crossing and uncrossing his legs. We crawl up to them slowly. Max keeps sniffing us. He probably thinks we've become dogs too. We bark. Woof. Woof. But when we reach the grownups we stop barking because they're so quiet. They do not say anything.

They're all staring at Daddy who is shining his shoes with his napkin. He holds the napkin stretched between his hands and rubs it over his shoes back and forth, back and forth. Soon they'll be like mirrors.

"I know it's late," Mummy says wrapping her arms around herself, "but would anyone like some tea? It's chilly this evening."

"I'm sure you feel the cold because you've lost so much weight," Granny says. "You used to have such a wonderful appetite. I've never seen you looking this way before."

"She doesn't look all that bad," Daddy says. He shoves the napkin into his pocket.

"Anyway," Granny says, looking up at the sky, "I think we should go in. It looks as if it's going to rain."

"I don't know," Daddy says. "I wouldn't be so pessimistic. I'd give it a chance if I were you. The sun might still come out. See—
it's struggling now." The sun appears once again as if my father could will it to come out when he wished.

"Well," Granny says, lifting her cuff and then raising her wrist to her face because she has trouble reading her watch. I run over. "Six thirty," I say.

"Just as I thought," Granny says. "It's almost time for our gin and tonics."

"I think we'll take a chance," Daddy says.

We watch Granny and Ethel walk towards the house. Granny rests her arm on Ethel's shoulder.

"Come here, my sweet," Mummy says. She brushes the hair away from my forehead. "You too, Alex. My goodness, you two are hot."

"We've been rolling in the grass," I say.

"Yes," Alex says, "we've been rolling in the grass." I pinch Al because she's always copying me. Mummy says she's a little echo.

We stare at the swallows swooping across the pool. They fly so low I expect their wings to touch the surface. Maybe Granny is right and it will rain.

"What have you two been up to?" Daddy says.

"Granny bought me a canoe," I say. "A big orange canoe and tomorrow we're going to go down the river."

"Daddy, do you want to come?" Alex says.

"I don't think there would be enough room for the three of us," he says.

"Yes, there is," Al says.

He looks over at Mummy. "Besides, we wouldn't want to leave your mother behind."

"Atchew, atchew," Mummy sneezes. She jumps up from her chair. "It must be the pollen in the air." We watch her walk across the grass. She walks very fast and the skirt of her dress swings from side to side. She runs into the house.

"I felt a drop," I say. "Granny's right, it's going to rain."

Clouds have gathered in the sky. There is only a small piece of blue sky left.

"No, no," Daddy says, "come here you two. I have a secret." We rush over. We love to hear secrets. I place my arm around Daddy's neck and then Al copies me and places hers around his neck too. She rests it on mine. I try to shrug her arm off, but then Daddy whispers, "I have something to tell you which is very very difficult to explain. You must listen carefully and try to understand." He turns his head from side to side to look at both of us. He pulls out his napkin and holds it in one hand.

"First," he says, "Tell me, do you like chocolate ice cream?"

"Oh yes," I say. "Very much."

"I like vanilla better," Alex says.

"Well," Daddy says, shoving his napkin back into his pocket. "Let's just pretend you both like chocolate and vanilla equally, I mean the same. Can you do that?"

"Oh yes," I say. "I'm very good at imagining."

"Now, this is the difficult part," he says. He takes out the napkin again and twists it between his fingers. "If I asked you to choose between the vanilla and the chocolate ice cream, it would be very, very, very difficult, assuming, I mean, if you liked both chocolate and vanilla the same?"

"Oh yes, it would," I say.

"Well," he says, "You see that's what's happened to me. I love your mother very much, but I also love another lady."

Perhaps my father's teasing. He loves to tease us. Sometimes he tickles us so much we pee in our pants. I giggle and look over my shoulder to see if he's laughing too, but he's staring down at the twisted napkin. Alex stares at me, as if to make up her mind. Her

49

mouth is wide open the way it is when Mummy tells us a story.

I watch the swallows swoop across the pool. They fly so low their breasts and sometimes the tip of one wing cut through the water, leaving a ripple which disappears immediately. There are many more swallows now. They seem to have all flown down from the vegetable garden, and their cries fill the air. Their cries seem too loud and the rest of the garden too quiet, too still, as if a spell had fallen on everything except for them.

"Aren't you coming in?" Mummy says, walking toward us, and we look up and realize that it has begun to rain. The rain comes down slowly, one big drop and then another big drop. I try to find a rhythm to the rain, plop ti plop, plop, but they're never even and the sound they make as they hit my arm or the chair or the earth is not the same.

"I've told them," Daddy says, letting the napkin drop to the ground.

Mummy stares at us, as if she could see it in our faces. Her forehead crinkles like a piece of paper, then she says, "Why?" She stares at Daddy's bent head. We wait for him to say something, but he continues to look down at the grass, at the folded napkin. She turns and I hear her gasp, as if she cannot breathe. She sobs and then she runs. She runs holding one hand to her chest, her skirt flying up in the back and Daddy jumps up from his chair and follows her. We watch him run after her. He catches up with her just before the stone steps. He grabs her elbow, but she breaks away. Over her shoulder, she shouts, "I thought we agreed," and Daddy stops and stands with his long arms hanging limply by his sides. He watches her disappear into the house, then slowly walks back towards us, passing his hand through his hair. Drops of rain have mottled his suit. "Shouldn't you be going in now?" he asks, as lightning strikes in the distance.

I walk slowly over to the pool, stare at the rain coming down hard now, tiny bursts of water which disappear as soon as they touch the green film covering the surface.

I let myself fall into the water, hear Al come in after me. The water is warm like tears, especially the top part, and smells of the rain and the grass and my clothes balloon and help me float but then they weigh me down and it's hard to swim. With my arms, I try to clear myself a clean path, but the grass closes in almost immediately. I swim round and round, then I float onto my back and look up at the sky.

"I think it's dangerous. Come out," Daddy says, but we continue to float as the storm becomes more and more fierce. Lightning strikes first white, then yellow, the garden lights up like the negative of a photograph.

I look over at my father only when I'm so cold, I'm shivering and Al's lips are blue. My father is sitting in a fold out chair. He sits without moving, looking down at his shoes, at the white-now-gray napkin lying on the grass. Drops of water slide down his forehead, along his nose. They accumulate at the tip and then they fall one by one onto his chin and then onto his shirt. His shirt has turned pink and his jacket and trousers have turned black and stick to his body in strange folds. His scalp shines between strands of wet hair. He looks up, and I see tears rolling from his eyes and landing on his hands. I look away.

***

Juliet stands in the middle of our room on the pale blue carpet with the white crosses. The sky is gray and the only light comes from the electric bulb in the corridor. She raises her Scottish kilt above her knees. At first, all I can focus on are her wide calves and her twisted feet. She puts one hand in the air and does a Scottish jig. She goes round and round the room, lifting one knee, then the other. Al's the first to laugh. I don't until Juliet drops her skirt and stands in her stockings and moves her hips from side to side, keeping her torso absolutely still. Then I can't help it.

***

We're sitting outside around the dining-room table covered with a white cloth Aunt Ethel and Granny embroidered the summer before. It was Daddy's idea to eat outside. The air is filled with the scent of the rain and the cut grass and every now and then when the breeze blows drops of water fall onto us. Al and I are wearing our best dresses, white dresses with tiny white butterflies. Juliet tied huge white bows to our hair. Al's fell off. Granny said we look like bridesmaids. Mummy looks like the bride because she's also wearing a white linen dress and a pearl necklace Daddy gave her.

She walks out of the kitchen holding a soufflé in a bowl. It's perfect, almost as high as a chef's hat. As she places the bowl on the

51

table, the soufflé wobbles and I'm afraid it will drop.

"Almost seems a shame to cut into it," Granny says.

"Yes," Daddy says. "Maybe we should all just look at it. A work of art."

Mummy cuts into the soufflé. She gives me a big helping, but she forgets that I like the sides of the soufflé, the crispy cheese parts.

It's very quiet. You can just hear the knives and forks against the plates, Ethel sipping her wine, water dropping from leaves and in the background the river.

I study the candles, the way they cast reflections across the white cloth and across people's faces. I hear Daddy tell Mummy how beautiful she looks and she says that candlelight is becoming to everyone.

"At my age not even candlelight will do it," Granny says.

"Did you grow up by candlelight?" I ask Granny.

She laughs and says she isn't that old.

"Maybe you should go on a cruise," Ethel suggests to Mummy and Daddy.

Daddy laughs, then brushes some crumbs off the table. "You think that's the solution," he says.

Juliet says she's never been on a cruise, just a hovercraft and she'll never do that again. I ask her what a hovercraft is and she says it's like a submarine. I don't think I'd like to go on a hovercraft. What if you get stuck down on the bottom of the sea and can't get out?

Al and I play touching each other's feet under the table. Then Daddy asks me to recite a poem I learned for school by Victor Hugo about a boy who died during the revolution. It's in French so neither Granny nor Ethel nor Juliet can understand it, but I recite it with as much feeling as I can, all the time staring at one corner of the white tablecloth. It's so sad, it makes me cry. The grownups are so moved they forget to clap and I can't tell if it's because of the poem or because of Mum and Dad.

Then Al and I ask to be excused. We float candles across the swimming pool.

Daddy turns on the gramophone and music drifts across the lawn. We watch Mum and Dad dance around the pool. I remember Mum telling me that Dad is not a very good dancer. He's always stepping on her feet. But tonight they seem to dance without any effort. Daddy holds Mum very tight and she rests her cheek against his chest. They're reflected in the water. You can see only pieces of them because of the big circles of floating grass. The grass specks Mummy's white stockings and white shoes and the cuffs of Daddy's trousers fill with grass.

We don't want Dad to dance with Juliet but when they do we can't help laughing. We ask her to do her belly dance, but she pretends not to know what we're talking about. Granny and Aunt Ethel sit and sip their gin and tonics. They wave to us from their blue fold-out chairs on the patio.

Four

In the morning I tiptoe up the stairs to my parents' room, past the boxer prints. Each boxer stands, arms lifted, knees bent, ready to punch. All three look alike. The only difference is in the color pants they wear: red, blue, and green. The house is silent except for the sound of a window opening and closing and the cries of birds flying to their nests under the eaves.

All I can see through the half-open door of my parents' room is the bottom corner of their bed and a section of the mantelpiece and the wall. I watch shadows shift, first one is on top then the other. The bed creaks. My father's orange heels come out from beneath the sheets. I cannot see my mother. Perhaps she's disappeared. I hear her moan. She is hidden beneath my father. He is suffocating her. I open the door further. My father is up on his hands.

I run back down the stairs and out the door, through the garden, across one narrow bridge, then another. The trees' reflections stretch all the way to the other bank, throwing shadows onto the grass. I pass snowballs, a cherry tree and a silver willow so tightly intertwined it's impossible to tell where one ends and the other begins. The wind dies and then picks up again, scattering petals and leaves. I watch the leaves float down the river until they meet weeds. The leaves churn round and round and some are sucked under and disappear. Sometimes I hear a flutter of wings and a strange cry and the long grass along the bank parts and a black moor hen flies up a few feet, then drops back down again. I think I hear my name called but there's no one, just the trembling of a branch. I continue but again I hear my name. I can't tell from which direction. I've reached the end of the bank where it narrows and there are bushes on either side and suddenly I feel as if the grass is rushing up at me and the trees are closing in and it's too quiet and I rush back along the bank as fast as I can.

Along the white fence the roses are drooping. Some have fallen apart, their petals scattered across the lawn. All that's left are their ugly heads. The birds are very loud. It's as if they've all come out to drink the rain. Then I hear Granny's dress. It makes a whispery sound. She places her hand on my shoulder.

"I'm feeling a bit tired this morning," she says.

"The roses are ruined," I say. "Finished."

"They'll come back," she says. "There will be even more soon. We just have to prune them."

She gives me a hug. I like the feeling of Granny's corset, firmer than anyone could possibly be.

"Gabriel," she says. "There are things I can't tell you because they're not for me to tell. Do you understand?"

"Yes," I say. I wonder if she means Daddy's lady. I wonder if his lady has boys. If he will like them better than us and go away.

"Why don't we go check on the vegetable garden?" She suggests.

"Okay," I say.

The garden glistens, drops of water lie in the seams of leaves. The geraniums have lost their petals. Each leaf is decorated by a round circle Granny calls a halo. We walk slowly across the stone patio. I stop to pull some moss between the cracks but drop it immediately when I see the pale gray beetles. Granny laughs. "They won't hurt you," she says. Slowly, we climb the hill to the vegetable garden and Granny leans quite heavily on my shoulder. When we reach the top, Granny says, "Shame!" The vegetable garden looks as if it has been shaken. The sweet peas have been stripped of their flowers, bits and pieces of their mauve petals are scattered across the earth and the grass. One of the cherry trees has lost a branch. We can see exactly where it broke off because of the clear oval circle.

Then we hear Mummy calling. She runs across the lawn. She's wearing a white nightdress with red ribbon threaded through the wrists and the hem. Her hair is down, and she's barefooted.

"He's leaving," she says. Her voice is faint.

"Oh dear," Granny says. She hugs Mummy, then presses me against her. For a moment, we stand at the top of the hill, staring at the trees bending in the wind. The top branches swirl round and round. They look like angry girls swinging their long hair.

Walking down the hill, we have to be careful because the grass is long and wet. Every now and then I slip. It makes me think of the time when Alex and I used to glide down the mountains. I wish there were mountains here.

Mummy says Daddy wants to have breakfast with us before he leaves, but I don't listen. I run to my treehouse. I sit on my bunk bed of logs and chew on a piece of grass. The sun struggles to appear through the clouds, but it can shed only now and then, a feeble light on the faded yellow buttercups along the river. I'm going to go down the river in my canoe. I'm going to go as far as I can. Maybe all the way to Estouy, where I'll buy some caranbar. They're my favorite sweets. Al likes to keep the wrappers. They're bright yellow with Caranbar written in purple.

"Gabriel," Juliet calls. She strides across the grass barefooted. Her hair blows this way and that. She looks angry, but I don't care. She can spank me with two shoes. Now she's standing at the bottom of my tree. If she's not careful, I'll pee on her.

"Come down at once," she says, her hands on her hips.

"But I—"

"Don't argue with me," she says.

She's always saying don't argue so I never get to say what I want.

Slowly, I climb down the tree. She grabs my hand.

"Your hands are freezing," she says. "You're to take a hot bath at once."

Perhaps I'll get pneumonia. When I'm sick, Juliet's very nice to me. She used to work as a nurse during the Second World War. I hope I get very ill and then she'll bring me hot lemonade with honey. She'll pat my pillows and sit beside me until I fall asleep.

"We've got to hurry," she says. "Your father's leaving and you're to have breakfast with him."

I like taking a bath in this tub because it has two levels. First, I sit with my knees bent on the bottom level, then when I get too hot, I sit on the top level. Juliet tells me about her family. How she has five brothers and how they all used to bully her. She says she used to try to impress them by falling onto her back without using her hands. Her brothers would call all their friends and then she would let herself drop onto her back. I can't imagine Juliet being bossed by anyone.

"I've got a treat for you," she says, pressing my hair down with one palm.

"What treat?" I ask.

"Well, this morning I weighed myself and I've lost two pounds.

Now that calls for a celebration, don't you think?"

"Are you going to buy a bikini?"

"Yes, as soon as I have you ready for breakfast, your granny and auntie and I are going into Malsherbes."

"What color will it be?"

"I haven't decided yet."

"Will you do a belly dance?"

"Perhaps, and maybe a Scottish jig. Off you go," she says.

I walk down the stairs counting each step, staring at the floor, first the wood then the white and black tiles then the gray flagstones in the dining room. I climb up onto my chair. Mummy and Al have already finished. There're just crumbs on their plates. These chairs are so high my feet don't touch the ground. I like brushing the velvet covering the seat.

The wind rustles the newspaper Daddy's reading. He puts it down but I don't look at him. I eat very carefully. I remember to use the butter knife. I put a piece of butter on my plate. I don't dip my bread in the egg. I wipe my mouth after I've eaten.

"You're very talkative," Daddy says. "You know, I'm not going to be here for very long. Your Daddy has to go away again."

I look down at my plate, and then I lean over the side of my chair and pretend to have dropped something. When I sit up, Daddy clears his throat. I look away from him through the window at the yellow flowers swaying in the wind.

I swing back on my chair, holding myself into place with my knees.

"Don't swing on your chair," Daddy says. "You could fall back and get paralyzed."

"I won't," I say.

"I didn't say you would necessarily. I'm just saying don't do it because it could happen."

"Are you going to Brussels?" I ask.

He passes his hand through his hair.

"Yes," he says.

"Are you going for very long?" I ask

"Not so long," he says.

"Did you bring us any presents?"

"No," he says. "But I will next time. Now remember your Daddy loves you very very much and you must be very good while

I'm away and look after your Mummy. Okay?"

He gets up. I follow him upstairs. First, he brushes his teeth, then he folds his pajamas and places them inside his shiny briefcase.

He stands in front of the mirror in his room and combs his hair. He tries several times to get a straight parting. "Shit," he says. "I don't know what's the matter with me today." I stand on tiptoes and stare over the mantelpiece into the mirror. I still can't see whether we look alike. I press the tip of my nose.

"It hasn't dropped yet," I say.

"What?" Daddy says, looking down at me, as if he just realized I was there.

"My nose," I say.

"You still have time," he says. "Remember, I was thirteen." He laughs and pats my head. "You look a little worried, Gabriel. Don't you want to have a handsome nose like your father's?"

"No," I say.

"That's not very nice," he says. "I think my nose would look great on your face."

He picks up his briefcase and hurries out of the room, glancing over his shoulder and brushing off his shoulder pad. "Where's your hat?" I ask.

"Which hat?" he asks.

"Your brown felt hat," I say.

"I don't know," he says.

"Will you get it back?"

"I hope so," he says.

Al and Mum are waiting at the bottom of the stairs. Daddy hugs Al and me and we watch Mum walk Dad to the car. We stare out the window of the front door. Mummy stands on tiptoes. She puts her arms around my father's neck and he lifts her up and up until her feet no longer touch the ground. He kisses her, then puts her down, and gets into his car. Mummy leans in. Perhaps she says, come back soon, or drive carefully. The car makes a loud vroom noise; goes through the white gate, up the hill before disappearing around the curve. Mummy stands for a moment longer, as if she could see further than us, beyond the bend where the car has disappeared.

Five

We're walking through the forest, down a narrow path that's like a green tunnel. The wind blows rustling leaves. White butterflies float from bush to bush. A rabbit shoots across the pathway. Max runs after it, disappearing into the bushes. Granny leads the way. She's holding the brim of her mauve hat with one hand. Al and I run up to her, then circle back to Mummy. She's wearing dark glasses that reflect the leaves and the branches and my face, but I don't recognize myself. My face looks big and my body tiny, like a genie. Luis is getting annoyed with us because we keep making him stop for bread. He's carrying the baskets. They're very heavy because we brought two baguettes, one pain de campagne, two bottles of apple cider, apples and pears and three different kinds of cheese: Granny's favorite boursin, brie and tallegio. We tread on Ethel's and Juliet's shadows as we go by.

We pass by caves where tramps are supposed to live. Mummy and Daddy used to take us for walks through here. Dad used to hold our hands and we would skip as high as we could. Once when Al and I went on a walk on our own I heard strange noises I thought belonged to a wild boar or a bear but later I found out that it was Daddy trying to scare us. Daddy has been gone for seven days and four hours and five minutes. I wish I had asked him whether his lady has boys. I'm sure she does. Twins. I hope they're ugly and stupid, but in my imagination they look just like him. Their hair is perfectly parted and they're first in their class.

Al and I are twins today. I'm wearing one of her special shirts with the pocket in the front. It's too small for me so I had to wear a T-shirt underneath. She lent me one of her hearing aids and I'm pretending I'm deaf. If Juliet asks me anything or Aunt Ethel I say, "I beg your pardon. I can't hear what you said." Then they talk louder and I tell them not to yell. They need to articulate. It makes Al laugh, but it really aggravates Ethel.

Each time we reach a fork in the path, Granny knows which way to go. She has the best sense of direction. She leads us to a clearing where trees and brambles and blackberry bushes form a circle. Over us, hidden behind clouds, the sun is like the moon.

Juliet and Aunt Ethel spread the blanket out, while Mummy helps Al and me blow up our canoe and Granny finds a bush of blackberries. She says she's going to make some jam. We sit down, but there's a terrible smell from the river. We're next to a stagnant part, so we have to move everything to the other side of the clearing where the river is clear and you can see stones and weeds fluoresce like green hair.

Al and I lie down beside Mummy in the sun. I run my fingers through her hair like a comb. I ask her to tell me about when she was a little girl. She tells us about the time she found a cat with ringworm. How a doctor came and she hid under the bed because she didn't want him to examine her.

"Did you ever come out?" Al asks.

"Eventually," she says. "They had to cut my hair."

"How come?" I ask.

"Because of the ringworm," she says.

"Did you ever get really, really ill and almost die?" I ask.

"When I got pneumonia," she says. "I remember drinking through a teapot."

"I'm hot," Al says. "Let's go for a swim."

"I'm going to lie here for a bit," Mummy says, closing her eyes. "Until I'm really roasting."

I stand and shift my weight from one foot to the other, but Mummy says, "Go on, darling. I'll only be a minute."

We swim for a long time with the sunlight glinting on the water. After, we climb up a tree and I see Granny placing her mauve hat on Mummy's head so that it shades her face while she's sleeping.

"A beautiful wedding," Granny says.

"Married awfully quickly," Ethel says.

We drop leaves but nobody notices.

"What about you, Juliet?" Granny asks.

I think she's going to tell Granny about her fiancé from the Second World War, but she talks about another man, a married man whose wife committed suicide. She had an affair with him. I think most grownups have affairs because I heard Mummy say that Granny had an affair too. Our grandfather was married when Granny met him. His wife committed suicide too. Suicide is when you kill yourself for love.

Juliet ends her story by saying, "He didn't marry me because I wasn't high class enough for him." She wanders off to pee. We see her squatting. We watch her fold a tiny piece of toilet paper. She's always scolding me for using too much toilet paper.

"Juliet's making pee pee," I say, but nobody listens. We watch her pull up her panties and pull down her skirt. She wanders off into the woods with her straw handbag over one arm.

"He'll be back," Ethel says.

"I wouldn't be a bit surprised," Granny says.

"Like a bad penny," Ethel says.

I turn up the volume of Al's hearing aid. Now all the sounds are amplified and the grownups' voices are garbled and I can't understand a thing. No wonder Al is tired by the end of the day. I turn the volume down.

Juliet sits back down in her chair. I wonder where she put the piece of toilet paper.

"Can we go down the river?" I ask.

They all look up.

"Well," Juliet says, "It's almost lunchtime."

"Please, please," I say.

In the end, the grownups agree and Granny says she'll come with us even though Ethel disapproves.

"Don't forget to give me your hearing aids," Juliet says. She wraps them in a white handkerchief and places them in her handbag.

There's plenty of room for the three of us. Al and I just have to scrunch up our knees.

As Juliet pushes the canoe from the bank, a gust of wind blows the clouds aside and the sun appears, turning the river silver. Ethel's beige dress melts into the trees almost at once and soon Juliet and Mum are splashes of blue and orange.

The river moves lazily here as if tired of having to twist in and out of curves. In some places the river is clear and shallow and we can see through the water to the stones lying on the floor of the river and the weeds look like long curly green hair. In other places, the river, sometimes quite suddenly around a bend, becomes murky and very deep and filled with mud and in these places the river smells. Perhaps that's why they call it l'oeuf, the egg, instead of its real name, L'Essone.

We drift by old mansions with lawns that stretch all the way to the river. An old woman all dressed in black runs alongside the river. She shouts, "L'année dernière deux enfants se sont noyés."

"Lulululu," Granny replies, imitating the woman's intonation in French. She waves her hand in the air, her gold bracelets jangling. We laugh, then both imitate Granny. I don't translate what the woman said, but I picture the two children drowned. In my imagination they are boys with dark hair and dark eyes.

We drift by silver willows. Our boat floats through their reflections. Granny leans back and slips her hand down her bodice, pulls out a cigarette, and lights it. "This is perfect," she says. She lets one hand trail through the water.

Her hair is so white.

"Look," Al says. "Look at the rabbit."

It stares at us without moving, as if fixed in place. Mummy once told us a story about people who looked over their shoulders and were turned to stone. I look ahead. I see another rabbit and another. They all sit in the same position as if rooted to the ground. I clap my hands but they do not move, their glassy eyes don't even flicker. I pass so close to one I could reach out and touch its ears.

"The rabbits are sick this year," Granny says.

I clap my hands and my claps echo. I'm glad Granny's with us or it would be spooky.

The current becomes swifter and we go faster and faster. Then around one bend the river flows slowly as if glad to rest. We lean over the sides of the boat and peer through the clear water. On the floor of the river we see blue bottles. At first we think they contain secret messages, but then we notice that the bottles are open. They have been placed so that their necks are facing the current. Through the blue glass we can see tiny trapped fish.

When we reach the clearing, we find Ethel asleep with her mouth wide open.

"There you are," Ethel says, waking up. "I thought you would never get here. It's past two o'clock."

"Have they really been gone that long?" Mummy says.

"You look like you had a nice rest," Granny says.

We sit on the blue blanket next to Mummy and Granny and eat

baguette with cheese. For dessert, we have our favorite: baguette with butter and powdered chocolate.

In the distance, we can hear Juliet and Luis laughing.

Suddenly, Juliet appears from behind the bushes on the other side of the clearing. She's wearing her new bikini. "Gabriel, Al," she shouts.

I look at Granny and she smiles and it seems like all her wrinkles disappear. "Go on, you two. I'll wait for you here."

We run across the grass towards Juliet. Her new bikini is all different colors. It reminds me of one of Al's drawings. "So what do you think?" she asks.

We stare at Juliet. We're not sure what to say. Her bikini is very different from Mummy's. The waist comes almost to her belly button and the top part is very pointy. It makes her breasts look enormous but I like the material. "Ooh Juliet," I say. "Can I touch it?"

It feels like the scales of a fish.

Luis stands by a tree smoking. He whistles, but Juliet ignores him and continues to walk through the grass on her tiptoes.

"Will you do your belly dance?" I ask. "You promised." She tiptoes a bit further so that we're out of sight.

She stands with her hands on her hips, and her face becomes calm. For a moment, she looks like she did in the photograph she showed me once where she was lying on a grassy bank with two men. She stretches her arms out and curls her fingers. It looks as if she's holding an invisible petticoat. She moves only the bottom part of her body, keeping the top completely still. She moves her hips from side to side, then from back to front. We giggle and roll on the grass. We laugh and laugh so hard I have to cross my legs to stop myself from peeing.

Then she says, "Did you know that I can faint on command?"

"Show us," Al says.

Juliet closes her eyes and drops on the grass. We giggle. I lift her arm. It falls back. We tickle her but she doesn't even twitch. We try to drag her across the grass but we can't because she's so heavy. "Luis," I say. "Come and help us."

Luis walks over. He drags her a little way and we giggle even more. "Juliet and Luis," we shout. "Juliet and Luis." We don't notice that it has started to rain until Ethel calls us. We leave Juliet lying on the grass with Luis holding her arms by the wrists.

Everyone hurries beneath a large tree. Aunt Ethel pulls out of her pocket a plastic hat for the rain. She offers it to Granny but Granny refuses. "Didn't I tell you it would rain?" Aunt Ethel says.

"What's a little rain?" Granny says.

"And where's Luis?" Ethel asks. "He always seems to disappear when you need him."

"He's with Juliet," I say, as Luis appears from behind a bush.

A few minutes later, Juliet reappears. She's pulled her clothes on over her bathing suit. But there's a leaf caught in her hair. I stare at the leaf, brown with a tiny bit of red along the edge, and she says, "What are you staring at?" and I say, "Nothing," because I can tell she's in one of her moods.

The rain comes down slowly but in big drops. I like the sound on the leaves and the ground. Al and I keep running from underneath the tree. Then Mum holds our hands and we dance round and round, with our faces tilted towards the sky. We sing and shout until we're soaked through. When it rains in Africa, Mummy says it sounds like thousands of people pounding their fists on the roof.

Ethel wants to stand for a bit longer under the tree, but Granny says there's no point because it's not going to stop raining so we start to walk. The tunnel of trees is dark now, filled with mist. Large snails appear and I stop to watch a pale pink one glide up a leaf. Luis says he would be happy to collect snails to cook for Granny, but she says not to mention the idea.

By the time we reach the dirt road, it's filled with mud. Our shoes keep getting stuck. Juliet's shoe comes off completely. She tells me to come so she can lean on me while she puts it back on. She gets annoyed when I suggest she ask Luis. She gets very mad when Al and I shout, "Juliet and Luis. Juliet and Luis have had a lovers' spat." We're so wet our clothes stick to our bodies. I can see Granny and Ethel's corsets through their dresses.

Then Granny trips.

I don't see it happen. All of a sudden she lies in the mud. Her face is very pale and her hair looks purple. I crouch on the ground and hold her hand. Juliet feels her ankle. She says she thinks it's not broken, just twisted. Luis bends over and lifts Granny. We follow him to the car. I insist on getting up front.

Inside the car it's dark and the sounds are muffled. There's just the tap tap of the window wipers and a clicking noise Mummy makes with her gold locket, pushing it in and out, reminding me of Daddy who used to put his hand on Mummy's hand and ask her to stop. It feels as if we're traveling through the air because it's so misty. I can't see the road or the trees. Now and then, when the mist parts I catch a glimpse of the river. It flows softly as if it were dreaming.

Even the house is hidden by the mist.

Granny says she does not need a doctor. Great-aunt Ethel says she thinks the man who owns the house across the way is a doctor. Juliet says it might be best for him to take a look, and Mummy says she'll walk to his house. She asks me if I would like to go with her. Al wants to come too, but Juliet says she has to stay with her. The doctor's garden doesn't have flowers, just a lawn and bushes that are perfectly trimmed. There's no wild part like our garden.

His house is modern. It's big and white and there are lots of windows and you can see right in. Once we saw the doctor in his underpants. It's the only modern house in the neighborhood, apart from the public housing apartment buildings just outside Malsherbes.

Mummy knocks lightly on the door. In the glass pane I can see her reflection. She looks very beautiful. Her hair is pulled back but it's curling and very full because of the rain. The orange jumper she's wearing has turned a deeper orange. I knock more loudly on the door. I bang until Mummy tells me to stop.

The door opens and a man with a very narrow face and big white hair appears. "Bonjour," he says. He talks so softly it's hard to hear what he says. "Vous êtes medecin?" Mummy asks. He nods. "Ma mère a tordu sa cheville," Mummy says. "Est'ce que vous pourriez venir l'examiner?" He says that he is not a general practitioner. He's a psychiatrist, but he would be glad to come over and take a look.

He goes back inside his house and comes out with a raincoat which he places over his head. He walks with tiny quick steps.

When we get to the house, Mummy says I should change out of my wet clothes. I don't want to, but Juliet appears and says I must. I watch the doctor walk with tiny steps to Granny's room. I do not like his narrow face. He makes me think of a fox.

That night I can't sleep for a very long time. I talk to my doll, the one Mummy gave me. She's made of rubber except for her head. Even her ears are made of rubber. She's only got one ear left and no eyes. I tell her not to worry. Everything is going to be all right. I promise to have her eyes fixed. Once I took her to a party and all my friends were giving their dolls a bath and I put my doll in the water, but when I pulled her out her eyes had popped in. I cried and cried and I thought Mummy would be mad but she said it wasn't my fault. Granny says that she knows a butcher who can fix my doll's eyes. I didn't know that butchers fixed dolls, but she said this one could.

Later in the night, I awaken to the sound of footsteps. The shadow of the cupboard door looks like a man. I don't move. I hold my breath. The cupboard door bangs shut and the curtain blows out into the room. Carefully, I push back my sheets and climb down from my bunk bed. I'm about to get into Al's bed when I hear Juliet slam her cup down on her bedside table.

Usually, she's reading an Agatha Christie with her glasses balanced on the end of her nose, her head leaning against the white wall above her bed. When she sits up, you can see a yellow circle on the wall. She gets very angry when I tell her she has a greasy head. She says everyone's head would leave a trace. Sometimes, she's not reading. She's sipping wine and looking up at the ceiling.

But tonight when I peer through the doorway, she's playing cards. She's playing patience. She's wearing her short, frilly, nylon, pink see-through nightdress. I open the door a little wider and the door creaks, but she does not look up. She's crying. The tears are dropping onto her cards, but she doesn't wipe them. I've never seen Juliet cry before. I wonder if she is thinking about her fiancé who died in the war. I imagine him thin and pale with long thin fingers. He lies on the grass like the soldier in Rimbaud's poem.

"Juliet," I say. She looks up at me but she doesn't seem to know who I am. She picks up one card then another but she doesn't move them to another pile; she just replaces them in the pile they were in. Then she says, "Go to bed."

"But I can't sleep," I say.

I walk over and sit down on her bed. "There are lots of creaks,"

I say. "Listen."

I strain to hear footsteps. I hear only the sound of moths beating against the lampshade, the river and the wind and Juliet's breathing, but then there's a loud bang and I squeeze Juliet's arm very hard.

"Ow," she says. "Now, I'm going to have a bruise."

"Did you hear?"

"It's just the wind," she says.

"Juliet, tell me about the Second World War some more," I say. Talking about the war always puts Juliet in a good mood.

"Go to bed," she says.

"Juliet, did you have a father and a mother?"

"Of course," she says.

"What was your father like?"

"He wore contact lenses," she said. "He was one of the very first people to wear them."

"What are they?" I ask.

"They're pieces of glass you put in your eyes to see better," she says.

I think it must be painful to wear pieces of glass in your eyes.

"He liked to eat cheese with maggots, right?" I ask.

"Yes," she says.

"Daddy likes to put vanilla ice cream in his express," I say.

She picks up the king of hearts and stares at it.

"What was your Mum like?"

"She used to sit darning our socks. Sometimes she wore a clothespin on the tip of her nose to make it thinner. She wanted to have an upturned nose." I feel like laughing, but I can tell that Juliet doesn't so I pull at the green cloth covering the walls, and she tells me not to so I wander over to the card table with the felt top where Juliet has laid out her puzzle. She's worked on it a little more, but you still can't tell for sure what the picture is going to be. All I can make out is a bit of the background which is dark green and looks like dirty water and something that could be a boat but would have to be pale green.

"Do you want to work on your puzzle?" I ask.

"It's much too late," she says.

"Would you like a tissue?" I ask.

"All right," she says.

67

I take a tissue from her tissue box on top of her chest of drawers. She blows her nose loudly, wiggling it from side to side. She needs another tissue and another. She tells me to bring her the trash can. Inside, I see her bikini. I don't ask her why she's put it there.

She sips her wine, pulls out another cigarette and lights it, then smokes, leaning outside her window. She doesn't say anything when I lean out with her. It's stopped raining but water drips from the roof onto our heads.

Six

In the morning, I slip into Granny's bed. I close my eyes and the sounds of her sleeping and the river mix so that at times I can't tell one from the other. I feel as if I'm floating. Perhaps it's because I spent so much time in the canoe yesterday. Granny said that for weeks after she's stepped off the QEII, the earth felt unstable, as if she was walking on the heaving deck of a ship.

I hear light footsteps. Mummy stands in the doorway. Her hair's all funny: it stands up on one side. The rims of her eyes are red and her white nightdress has a stain down the front. She slips into bed next to me. She has to lie on the very edge because we don't want to wake Granny. "Talk to me," Mummy says. I have so much to tell her. I could talk all day. First, I tell her how I wish I didn't have to go back to school in September. She says not to worry about school. We have quite a few weeks until then. Besides, she says, you did much better at school this trimester. I tell her about how I hope to get the cross of encouragement next trimester. I almost got it last trimester, but they gave it to another girl. There are three kinds of crosses: croix de première is for the best student, croix de seconde is for the second best, croix de troisième is for the third best and then there's the croix d'encouragement which is for the student who has made the most effort. I have never had any of the crosses. They look just like general's crosses and you attach them to your sleeve. You only get to wear them for three weeks, then you have to earn them all over again. You can also earn blue, red, and yellow ribbons during exams. I imitate all my teachers and Mummy laughs very hard. Her laugh is the best laugh. It's high pitched and goes higher and higher. When she laughs in the cinema, everyone laughs with her. She laughs especially hard when I imitate my teacher making the distinction between un accent grave and an accent aigu. It wakes Granny up.

"Hello, darling," Granny says. "It's good to hear you laugh. How are you feeling?"

"How are you feeling?" Mummy asks.

"Not too bad," she says. "A bit sleepy." She touches the cat on her head. "I thought I felt a weight pressing me down." Tiger jumps off her head onto the carpet and runs out the door.

Granny closes her eyes and we continue to talk in whispers.

I ask Mummy if Granny is going to have to go to the hospital and she says she doesn't. The doctor said she's just twisted her ankle.

"Have you ever been in a hospital, Mummy?" I ask

"To have you and Al," she says. She tells me how when she was in the hospital she had to press a button and say in a loud voice over a loudspeaker that she had to peepee, but she felt so embarrassed that she held it in for as long as she could. My Mum was only seventeen when she had me. She asked Daddy to change her room twice. First, she wanted to be in her own private room but then she got lonely, so she asked to be with other women but they all made comments about how young she looked so then she asked to be put back in a private room.

The light on the blue-green mohair blanket is very bright. It's warm and I ask Mummy if she would like to go for a swim and she says that's a lovely idea.

We tiptoe out of Granny's room, through the living room which is just as it was our first morning here. The air is cool and drifts through the open windows, rippling the blue curtain hems.

We run out the door across the wet lawn, let our nightdresses drop onto the grass, and dive naked into the pool.

The water is cool and smooth next to my skin and I float on my back. I look up at the sky and wonder what my father is doing.

When I go back to Granny's room, she's hobbling around in the nude. Granny loves to walk around naked. Her skin is all loose and floppy. It hangs in folds and is very white.

We tiptoe through Ethel's room to get to the bathroom, but Aunt Ethel awakens.

"Really, Will," she says, sitting up. She does not approve of Granny walking in the nude.

"I'm going to help Granny with her bath," I say.

We fill up the tub very high and put in lots and lots of rose bubbles. Granny holds onto my shoulders as she slowly lowers herself into the water. I pass a big sponge over her back. She has lots of brown freckles and tiny red dots. I ask her what the red dots are and she says they're burst blood vessels.

"Lovely, lovely," she says, scooping water and throwing it over her shoulders so that it splashes her back.

"What are we going to do today?" I ask.

"Well," she says, "I'm not going to be up to much, but you can play in your treehouses. Or you can do some knitting."

After her bath, Granny sits in the armchair that matches the waterlily couch. She lets me sprinkle her with baby powder. I put on lots and lots of powder until she says, "That's enough, dear. You're putting some even in my hair." I laugh and tell her that was what they did in the old days. Then she asks me to pass her one of her paper panties. I love her paper panties. They're pink and white and come in a long string of plastic bags connected to one another. She lets me have a pair.

I watch her as she bends over and carefully places one foot, then the other, quite swollen now, through each leg hole of her panties. Her fingers tremble and I want to reach out and help her but I'm not sure she'd want me to. I remember the way she gets annoyed when Luis tries to help her out of the car by swinging her legs over the side. She breathes heavily and straightens up. She's not going to wear her corset today, just her cream dress.

She's just pulled it on when there's a knock on the door and Juliet and Ethel come in. Juliet sits down on the couch and places Granny's foot on her lap. Her foot is so small you'd think it was a little girl's if it weren't for the blue veins and the way her bones stick out. We watch Juliet tie a beige bandage around Granny's foot. She says you mustn't do it too tight or too loose. In a few days she'll let me do it.

Mummy and Al come into Granny's room and we all stand around Granny and she says she's very happy to have her family au complet, then she leans back and closes her eyes.

Ethel says we must leave her room. "Have a nice day off," Granny says to Juliet. I beg Mummy to go with us in the canoe. It's really fun because the river is very full and the current strong. She says she'll come as long as we stay within earshot of the house. I wonder if she's waiting for a telephone call from Daddy.

We spread our towels on the bottom of the canoe and Mummy

and I sit at either end with Al in the middle. I ask Mummy to tell me about when she was a little girl. Her father died when she was only seven years old and she and her sister moved from their big house into a tiny apartment with Granny. She says she was very spoiled. She was Granny's favorite because she was the littlest one.

Her sister would beg her not to get on her bed, not even to touch it with one finger, but Mummy would and her sister would smack her and then Mum would run to Granny and tell on her. But sometimes Mum had a bad time, especially when her cousin Heather would come over. She was four years older than Mum and two years older than my mother's sister. They would tease Mum by saying, "Where is Claire? Where is Claire? She's down in the garden picking her nose," and she would say, "But I'm here. I'm here." My Mum says she still feels like that sometimes because we're foreigners in France. She says it's different for us because we're little, but I don't think that's true. When I'm at school and the teacher asks us a question about America, she always turns to me. She says, "Gabriel is American. She must know." And then when I don't know, everyone is disappointed. "But I haven't been there since I was five," I say. "My mother is South African." No one will believe that Mum is South African because they think that all South Africans are black but they're not.

When Mummy stops talking, she says she really must get some practicing done. We watch her walk through the grass and across the patio and into the house. Soon the sound of her practicing drifts out onto the lawn and the water. Al and I continue to float in the canoe. We see the doctor trimming hedges. We see nests with blue or green or cream speckled colored eggs, but we do not touch them. We know we must not. When I was younger, I took some eggs and put them near the radiator. I thought they would hatch and I could have baby birds, but Granny explained that the mother has to sit on top of them to keep them warm. We drift all the way to the green bridge. We stare at the water rushing towards the dam. We can feel the pull on the canoe. Al says we should let the canoe go down, but I say no, and we turn around. We can't row because the current is too strong, so we take the canoe out and then we let out the air and fold it up and I carry it under one arm until we reach our treehouses.

We pretend to be soldiers and use our towels for capes, blackberry juice for blood. We've been wounded at war. I wrap my towel around one arm. Al wraps hers around her waist and drags a leg. We pick up two sticks we pretend are sabers. The grownups are the distant enemy. We're on the look-out for Daddy. I tell Al how Granny and Ethel said he was bound to show up. Like a bad penny, Ethel said.

"What's a bad penny?" Al asks.

"It's a penny that's no good," I say.

"What's a penny that's no good?"

"I don't know," I say. "I guess it's a penny that's bent or crooked or something."

In front of the house, we see Luis washing his car. Large soapy bubbles glide across the car and drip down onto the gravel. Al and I like the wet stones, but as soon as they dry they don't look beautiful anymore. We watch Luis dip a large brown sponge in a red bucket. He shows us the correct way to rub the car: in circles. He says we can climb into the car, as long as we don't put our shoes on the cream seats. Luis's skin is the same color as the seats. We take turns looking at the photograph of his two boys which dangles from the rear view mirror. They look exactly the way I imagine Daddy's lady's twin boys. They have dark hair and dark eyebrows and they're wearing the same outfits.

He hoses the car down while we're inside. I tell Al we should pretend we're in a boat that's sinking. This is what it would look like. We scream but no one can hear us. Luis has fallen outside the boat. He's drowning. Through the water, we can see only bits of the house. The ivy leaves are seaweed, the house itself an old buried boat. Our little boat is soon going to sink beside it. We try to see who can hold their breath the longest. Al wins. She almost faints.

When Luis has finished hosing the car, we get out. The car gleams in the sunlight and Al and I can see our watery reflections in the door. Luis is singing a Spanish song. Las Campagna della Laura. Las Campagna della Laura. Uno. Dos. Tres. I ask him if his boys miss him and he says that since he's gone most of the time, they're used to it. But I think he's wrong. In my imagination, I picture them weeping, as they wave from behind a window.

Luis scratches his ear with one finger and asks us if we think Miss Juliet is ready.

We run upstairs. We knock on her door, but she doesn't answer. There's not a sound, then I hear footsteps. The door opens a crack.

She's in her nightdress.

"Yes?" she asks.

"Luis is waiting," I say.

"For what?" she says.

"For you," I say. "For your day off."

"Well," she says. "Tell him I've changed my mind."

"Okay," I say.

"Okay," Al says.

She closes the door and then we hear her stumble into something, her bedside table, perhaps.

Seven

In the night the phone rings. It rings and rings, then I hear Mummy's piano, but when I tiptoe to the music room there's no one. I hear Juliet singing. Her voice drifts in and out of my dreams.

When I awaken, I think I can see water reflected onto the white wall in our bedroom, but it's the shadows of leaves. I jump down from my bunk bed and race down the stairs through the living room. I'm afraid I'm too late to fix Granny's bandage. Juliet promised I could do it on my own today.

Light filters between the curtains, cutting through the grownups. Granny is already dressed. She's sitting on the couch holding Mum's hand. Ethel stands with her back to me, folding Granny's clothes.

"There you are," Granny says. "I was waiting for you."

First, I rest Granny's foot on a pillow and massage cream into her foot. The cream has a strange mediciny smell that makes Mummy sneeze. I unwind a fresh strip of tan-colored bandage from the roll Juliet keeps on top of Granny's medicine case and cut a piece. I wrap it around Granny's foot and ankle, doing it exactly like Juliet, starting with Granny's instep. I tie the bandage in place with a small clip. All the time I'm doing it, I can feel Ethel and Mummy watching me. It takes me much longer than Juliet, but Granny says I've done a fine job.

"Wouldn't it be nice to be ten again?" Mummy says.

"If you knew what you know now," Ethel says.

"Don't be silly. You're still so young," Granny says, turning to Mum. "You're a baby."

"I'd like to be grown up," I say.

"It's always like that," Mummy says. She tucks a strand of my hair behind one ear.

We watch Ethel fold Granny's handkerchiefs. She places them in a pink bag with a transparent white cover embroidered with flowers. Granny bought it when she was in Switzerland.

"I don't know what to do," Mummy says.

"You must be firm," Granny says. "At the very least tell him you need a few days to think it over."

"It's not like it's the first time," Ethel says. "And look what happened."

"Well, it is a bit different," Mummy says. She whispers something in Granny's ear.

I know they're talking about Daddy. I want to ask them but Juliet and Al appear in the doorway. The top of Al's head is all wet. I can tell that Juliet has tried to flatten her hair.

"And how are we today?" Juliet asks.

"Better," Granny says.

Juliet looks at Granny's bandage. "Not bad at all," she says to me. "Would anyone like tea?"

Everyone says yes. I like my tea with lots of milk and six tablespoons of sugar. Juliet is always telling me how bad it is to have so much sugar. Ethel doesn't take sugar. She continues to fold and lets me place Granny's silk petticoats in a drawer. Mummy looks tired again. She's wearing the same blue jumpsuit she wore yesterday. Al leans against her legs.

Then there's a knock on the door. Ethel and Granny and Mummy look at each other.

"Do you think—" Ethel says.

"Surely, not—" Granny says.

"He wouldn't—" Mummy says. "Gabriel and Al, go and see who it is."

We run to the front door. I think it might be my father, but it's the doctor. He's dressed in a tight blue suit and he's carrying a brown briefcase. I let him into the entrance hall and run back to Granny's room.

"It's the doctor," I say.

"What a relief," Ethel whispers.

Mummy laughs.

Mummy and Ethel walk into the living room. Bonjour. Bonjour. Bonjour.

Max barks very loudly. I wonder if he will jump up onto the doctor. Al and I make faces. We don't like doctors. They give injections. They chop up people and they touch the dead.

Through the doorway of Granny's room, we watch him. He is very old-fashioned and bends over and kisses the back of Mummy's

hand, saying, "Enchanté" He's going to expect us to curtsy, I bet.
Later, Al and I imitate the way he says, *Enchanté*

Max growls at him and Mummy has to hold him back. She asks
me to come get him and say bonjour to the doctor. I drag my feet
and look down at the floor, then hold out my hand and say bonjour.
His handshake feels like water. I tell Max to come but he won't. I
wish he would pass wind. He won't come until I give him a piece
of bread, then he follows me, his short tail wagging. He used to
have a long tail, but he's the kind of dog that has to have a short
tail so they cut some of it off. I don't understand why some dogs
have to have short tails and some don't.

The doctor talks to Mummy but we can't hear what he says
because he talks so softly. Mummy looks surprised. She blushes
and touches the back of her hair as if she just remembered she had-
n't combed it. She laughs, then says, "oui." He walks over to
Granny's room with tiny quick steps.

"I jeest wanted to see how you are faring," he says. "After three
days, the swelling should be down."

Al and I giggle at his French accent. Al can tell it's funny by the
way his lips and tongue move.

He undoes the bandage slowly and examines Granny's foot. He
asks who did the bandage and I say I did. "Well, done," he says. I
try not to smile.

He leaves his phone number with Mummy, and tells her that if
there is a problem to give him a call. "I hate to be any trouble,"
Mummy says.

"No trouble at all," he says. "My pleasure."

She offers to pay him but he won't hear of it. He tells her that
after all, we are neighbors.

Juliet enters the living room with a silver tray, teacups, and a
teapot.

Ethel asks him if he would like to stay for a cup of tea, but he
says no, thank you. He has business to attend to.

Mummy walks the doctor across the gravel yard up to the white
gate.

"What a nice man," Ethel says. "So polite."

"Yes," Juliet says.

"I seem to remember Mme Daudiet telling us something," Ethel says. "He used to be married."

"The wife—" Juliet whispers in Ethel's ear.

"Poor thing," Ethel says. "Somehow it seems worse when it happens to a man."

Al and I run upstairs and jump on our beds. We jump as high as we can. We try to touch the ceiling, but Juliet tells us not to so we lie on our beds with our hands behind our heads. We sing at the top of our lungs. "Les Anges de la campagne ont entonnés l'hymn des cieux."

"You're to stop immediately," Juliet says, standing barefooted in the doorway.

"There's nothing wrong with singing," I say.

"Don't argue," she says.

"I can smell your feet from here," I say.

"Don't you be rude," she says. She stands on my bed and I tell her to get off because she's going to make my sheets smelly. "Stinkpot," I call her. She beats me with her shoe, but I don't cry.

Al and I escape to Mummy's side of the house. She's taking a bath. I tell her that Juliet has been beating me with her shoe, but Mum won't believe me. She says that Juliet would never do such a thing. "She did too," Al says. "I saw her."

"What did you do?" Mummy says.

"I said her feet are smelly and it's true," I say. "They smell like brie."

"That wasn't very nice," Mummy says.

"But she shouldn't hit me with her shoe," I say.

Mummy says why don't we get in her bath. It's a big bath because Daddy is so tall he wouldn't fit in a normal one. I wonder if his lady has a big tub or if he has to sit all scrunched up. Our tub is big enough for a whole family. We make the water as hot as we can bear it. We go bright red and sweat and then we run cold water. We pretend to be opera singers. "Oh my darling, I love you so much." We sing in French because it sounds more romantic. "Mon amour. Je meurs d'amour pour toi."

We all sound terrible, not just Al, but Mum and me too because neither of us has a good voice and because we exaggerate. I try to do it the way I heard a real opera singer sing once when I went for my ballet class, and it makes Mum and Al laugh even harder.

After our bath, we go out into the garden and lie in the hammock with Mummy. Al brings her white blanket with the blue flowers. Mum brings her poetry book by Lamartine and I bring the box of dried fruit Granny brought all the way from South Africa. It's special dried fruit, crushed and then molded into squares, dusted with sugar and wrapped in waxing paper. They're all different colored squares: some are pink, some are green, some are orange, blue, or purple. I like the red ones best. I've asked Granny to send me two whole boxes for my next birthday.

Al asks Mummy to tell us about the times she was naughty, and Mum tells us about the time that she and her sister smoked a whole pack of cigarettes in the back of a car. They were so sick Mum hasn't tried a cigarette since. Daddy smokes cigarettes. I like the smell in his car in the leather seats. But I don't tell Mum what I'm thinking. Instead I ask her what her Dad was like. She says she doesn't remember him very well because he died when she was seven. He was very good at mathematics, but she's hopeless at it. "I'm no good either," I say.

"I'm no good either," Al says.

"Yes, you are," I say. "It's so annoying, Mum, the way she always copies me."

"You should take that as a compliment," Mum says.

I hate it.

I ask Mum to tell me again the story of how she met Dad even though I know it all by heart. She was in Italy going out with an Italian boy called Enrico and he introduced her to his best friend, our Daddy, and Daddy fell madly in love with her. He followed her all the way to Salzburg in his white Lancia. He went back to university but he couldn't bear being away from her so he flew over to France where Mum was learning French and then they both flew to South Africa where they got married. Daddy's father refused to speak to him. He didn't want Daddy to marry Mum because he said he was too young.

We spend all morning in the hammock and we eat all the dried fruit except for the green squares.

When we go back inside the house, Granny and Ethel and Juliet have already sat down for lunch. Granny smiles at us. She takes Mummy's face between her hands and kisses her on both cheeks.

"Did you wash your hands?" Juliet asks. We rush to the sink and Mummy follows us and we get the giggles because she says that she feels like a little girl herself the way Juliet speaks to her. She says we'd better eat or she'll get into trouble and Juliet will give her a spanking.

Al and I take huge servings but then we have trouble finishing. Every time I look up from my dish, Juliet is watching me. I remember reading about a girl hiding her steak in a napkin, but I don't know how she did it. Once, at school, we had to eat liver and I cut it up into little pieces and my friend Catherine and I flicked the pieces under somebody else's table.

After lunch, Mum says she really must get some piano practicing in. Al and I march to our treehouses where we play soldiers again. Our wounds are more serious than we thought. "Not just superficial wounds," I tell Al. I have trouble explaining the meaning of the word superficial. In the end, I tell her we're missing an arm or a leg. We're under siege and there are only muskrats to eat. We're up on the rampart of a castle. I tell Al she has to be vigilant or else the enemy will invade. Soldiers who fall asleep while on duty are shot. I'm a general like our grandfather. He fought in the white army. Daddy says we're descendants of white Russians. Xorosho, I say to Al.

I climb up a branch and stare at the wild field. I think I see my father. He's standing on the other side of the river. I recognize his hat and the color of his shirt. I call out to him. "Hey, Daddy. Daddy," but he drops out of sight and there's just the sun flickering across the river. I tell Al not to tell anyone. Cross Your Heart and Hope to Die, I say.

***

In the night, Juliet's breath falls across my face like a shadow. She mutters something and tiptoes across the room. "Ow," she says as she trips on my shoes. I wait until she's left our bedroom before climbing out of bed.

I peer through her open door. Clothes and books are strewn across the floor. Tangerine peels lie in a pile by her bed. She's sitting on the carpet with her legs spread apart, her back to me. "Juliet, I can't sleep." I tiptoe up to her. "I saw Daddy today." She does not turn. She does not seem to have heard me. A red cardboard box lies between her legs.

"What's in there?" I ask.

"Go to bed," she says, without turning round. She tries to open the box but for some reason she has trouble. She keeps fumbling with the ribbon, then she hurls the box across the room. I walk over and pick it up.

"Don't you touch that. I'm warning you."

I pass it to her.

She holds it and looks at it as if she's forgotten what she wanted it for. She hands it back over to me. I untie the ribbon and open it. Inside are cards and photographs of children.

"Pass that to me," she says. She places the photographs in a row as if she were playing solitaire. She picks up one card and lets me hold it. It's a drawing of an orange cat with a boy's face. "Dear Julia," I read. "I miss you and think of you fondly."

"Is your real name Julia?" I ask.

"Of course not," Juliet says. "That's just what he called me."

I pick up a photograph of a smiling girl with big white teeth. On the back it says how she wants Juliet to see what she looks like without braces. Juliet grabs the photograph from me.

"What did I say about touching? I don't know why she sent this to me. I've never known her with braces."

"What was her name?"

"Jenny, or was it Melanie?" she says. "Something like that."

"Who was your favorite?" I say.

"I don't have favorites," she says.

"Yes, you do. You told me once your favorite was Andrew. He was perfect and never did anything naughty."

Sometimes I was Daddy's favorite. Sometimes Al was. We never know.

"D'you think Daddy's coming back?"

"I have no idea," she says.

"What happened to your bikini?" I ask, wondering if she took it out of the trashcan or if she threw it out the window.

"What do you mean what happened to my bikini?"

I picture it floating down the river. Perhaps it's met up with Daddy's brown felt hat. I imagine the hat and the bikini swirling.

There's a tiny flash as the bulb in her lamp burns out and we're in the dark. Clouds drift in front of the full moon. At times I can see Juliet very clearly, but then it's too dark. I lie on my stomach over her red poof.

Eight

Light slides along the hem of the curtain like a snake. First Mummy's in the sunlight, then she isn't. She's wearing a new cream dress with buttons like caramels. She turns her head from side to side so that she can catch sight in the mirror of her hair twisted in back. Mummy's profile is perfect. She has a high forehead and a small straight nose, slim lips. Mummy makes me think of the heroines on the covers of Granny's novels. Daddy used to tease her and say that she has thin lips while he has big generous lips. He said my lips are like his.

"What do you think? Do you think I look all right?" Mummy asks, swirling around, flaring her skirt.

I remember Daddy saying "you look lovely. Doesn't she look lovely."

"You look nice," I say, staring at my own reflection: my long thin arms and legs, my broad face. I hunch a little more, remembering how my father would always tell me to stand up straight. "If you continue like that," he would say, "You'll be like the hunchback of Notre Dame."

Mummy has perfect posture. Her back is very straight and she holds her head up high.

"Do you really think I look all right?" Mummy asks.

"You look lovely," I say. "The woman in the store said you look just like Grace Kelly."

Mummy smiles, then stares off into the distance as if she remembered something. Her hands flutter to her hair.

"I feel so old," she says. "Isn't it funny I remember thinking I would never live past twenty-five and here I am twenty-seven."

"But you look very young," I say. "That man in the café said he thought we were sisters."

"Oh, that was just flattery."

"Mummy, why do you dye your hair?"

"Oh darling. I already explained that to you. I've been doing it for years. It's not your Mummy's fault that she went white at twenty-five. It reminds me of the time I cut my hair. I came to pick you up at school and you burst into tears."

"But why did you dye it a different color?" I ask. "Why did you dye it yellow?"

Mummy laughs. "I hope it's not yellow. It's supposed to be blond."

"Blond," I say.

"For a change," she says. "Oh darling, don't be difficult. Anyway, there's something I have to tell you. Your Mummy is going on a date."

I stare at her shoes. They're cream sandals with straps that tie around the ankle.

"Imagine, I haven't been on a date since I was seventeen," Mummy says. "I'm not sure I'll know what to do. I'm not sure I should be going at all."

"Of course, you should," Ethel says from the hallway. She peers into Mummy's room. "I was just coming to tell you that it's almost seven— exquisite. Doesn't she look exquisite?" Ethel repeats, looking over her shoulder.

What a silly word. Exquisite. An exquisite cup of tea. An exquisite dress. An exquisite idiot.

"Yes, you look very pretty tonight," Granny says, appearing beside Ethel. "Go on. It will do you good to get out."

"What if he calls?" Mummy says.

"We'll tell him you're on a date," Granny answers.

"You wouldn't," Mummy laughs.

"Who's your date?" I ask.

"The doctor, darling."

"I thought he came to see Granny."

"Well, he did," Granny says. "But that was just a pretext to see your mother."

"When did he ask you?" I say.

"Yesterday," Mummy says.

"But he doesn't know you."

"It's just a date," Granny says.

"But he's old."

"Not that old," Mummy laughs. "He's like me. His hair went white prematurely."

"I'd say he's around forty," Ethel says.

I think I see a darker part in the carpet where Max peed.

"You're not going to pout, are you?" Mummy says.

I run from her room down the stairs through the living room, out the house, past the burnt remains of the old house, over a bridge and along the bank of willows where the grass has grown so long it reaches my knees.

I climb up my tree and stand on my bunk bed of logs. I narrow my eyes and stare at the field in the distance. I keep my eyes fixed on the tops of the dry stalks.

"Hey," Al says. "Want to play soldiers?"

"Go away," I say.

"Why?" she demands.

"Because."

"Because why?"

"I don't feel like seeing your face," I say.

She plays with her hearing aids, wiggling one, then the other, and looking up at me.

"Stop," I say.

"What?"

"That noise."

"My ears are itching," she says.

I watch her walk slowly along the bank of silver willows. She's holding a stick and wacking any flowers she passes. I can hear her sing-song a funny song a friend of hers taught her. "Talia bata wana marie. Shili Shanta. Ona marie." Her voice grows more and more faint until all I can hear is the wind and the water.

From beneath a log, I pull out a pair of binoculars and an atlas I found in the attic. I place my finger on Brussels, wondering if we could go by boat. I trace one river, then another. I picture a gray city with buildings enveloped in mist. Even the sound of church bells is muffled. Cats and dogs are quiet. Children don't speak. I peer through the binoculars. They belonged to my father. They're brown and one of the lenses is cracked but I can see through the one lens. I bring the line of stalks into focus. I stare and stare until the eye I've kept closed aches and I have to switch eyes. There's no one. Just an ugly moor hen which swoops into sight, then drops out of my view. I train the binoculars on the house. The vines seem to have grown even more this summer. There's almost no stone showing. The vines flutter in the wind and look like water from this distance. I think I see Mummy peering out her window.

I swing down from a branch and race along the bank of silver willows, but when I get to Mummy's room she's already gone. There's just a trace of her perfume in the air.

I walk slowly to the stairs. The grownups look different from up here. I can see the tops of their heads.

I cross the living room over to Granny. The string of pearls she wears around her neck stands out even in the shade. She says that if you don't wear pearls they become dull. I lean against the arm of her chair and watch her knit. I like the clicking sound her needles make. She goes very fast and she hardly looks down.

I stare up at the painting in dark browns and blues of the little girl whose head is too big for her body. In one hand, she holds a red string that's tied around a cat's neck. She doesn't look like a little girl, more like a grownup with a short body. Her hair is parted in the middle and curled at the bottom.

"Gabriel," Juliet says. "Why don't you find Alex?"

"Oh no," I say.

"Gabriel," Juliet says.

"I saw my Daddy," I say.

"Don't lie," Ethel says.

"I did. I saw him in the wild field. He was wearing a blue shirt with gold cufflinks."

"Did he talk to you?" Ethel asks.

"He waved," I say.

I look at Granny, but she doesn't say anything. She continues her knitting.

I run out into the garden, yell "Al. Al." She's walking along the bank of dahlias with Luis. He's cutting flowers and she's placing them in a basket. I run up to them and ask who the flowers are for, but Al says it's a secret.

When I peer into the living room, the grownups are drinking their gin and tonics. I tiptoe to my bedroom and lie down on my bunk bed.

"Dinner's ready," Juliet says. She wipes her wet hands on her apron.

"I don't feel hungry," I say.

"I don't care what you feel. You're to come down at once.

Don't you be difficult tonight, Gabriel. I'm warning you. I'm in no mood to put up with any of your nonsense."

"Juliet," I say. "I don't feel well. I have a terrible stomachache." She marches out. Suddenly, I really do have a terrible stomachache. It's like the ones I sometimes get before going to school. Mummy took me to lots of doctors, but they couldn't find anything wrong.

I wish Al were here. I'd ask her to jump on my stomach. It's the only thing that makes the pain go away. The grownups voices drift upstairs from the dining room. Granny calls for me to come but I tell her I'm not hungry. I can hear the knives and forks across the plates. I imagine my father walking through the wild field. He pushes the stalks aside. He's not scared of stepping on snakes. His head goes from side to side and he sings a Russian song.

Later I slip into Granny's bed. She's been going to bed earlier and earlier. It's only eight o'clock. Her room is filled with a pink light. I curl up next to her and rest my head on her shoulder. My stomach still hurts me. She waits for me to suggest we read. Then she pulls out her book which has a bright cover with a picture of a man sitting on a horse. In front of the hero, sitting sideways, is the heroine wearing a navy blue cloak trimmed with ermine. The heroines are all like Granny. They come from very poor families and then they marry millionaires. They're small and delicate and they have the tiniest hands and feet. At first the heroine and the hero don't understand each other and the hero is mean to the heroine, but in the end the heroine makes the hero change and they live happily ever after. While Granny reads, I stare at the squares of pink on the white wall. Gradually, they get smaller and smaller until they disappear and it's almost dark. But it doesn't seem to bother Granny. She continues to read. She reads with a lot of expression. Sometimes, when there's dialogue she takes on the man's voice and the woman's and it makes me laugh. Occasionally, we hear a creak as Juliet walks overhead.

I don't remember Granny turning off the light. I must have fallen asleep listening to her voice because when I awaken it's dark. The light coming through the windows looks blue. My tummyache's gone. I don't hear Granny snoring. I lean over her and the white of her eyes glows. "Granny, are you awake?"

"Yes, dear. I've been listening to you sleep."

"You look strange," I say. "The whites of your eyes glow."

"Yours do too," she says, leaning over me. "Where's that cat?"

"Under the sheets by my feet," I say.

Then I hear a car drive across the gravel. I tell Granny and she switches on the light. The front door opens and we hear Mummy's quick footsteps.

"Are you awake, mother?" Mummy asks.

"Yes, " Granny says.

"Me too," I say.

"It's awfully late," Mummy says.

"Yes," Granny says. "It's almost two o'clock. I'm glad to see you back safe."

Mummy hugs Granny and kisses me on the head.

"I'd better let you sleep. I've kept you up late as it is." She tip-toes out of the room.

"She looked happy," I say.

"Yes," Granny says.

I stay awake for a long time, listening to Granny's snores, staring at the blue light coming from the windows because we didn't close the shutters.

Nine.

We're in the kitchen sitting around the white table that wobbles if anyone leans on it. We're all in our nightdresses, except for Mummy. She's wearing a navy blue skirt and a white shirt Daddy says makes her look like a schoolgirl. She went into Malsherbes early and bought croissants and brioches.

Juliet's standing by the stove cooking bacon.

"I wonder if we should put on a light," Ethel asks, as the kitchen falls back into the shade but then it's light again and the copper pans and the yellow counters gleam. The sun can't make up its mind. It keeps pushing through the clouds and then slipping back.

"I think we're all right," Granny says.

I hear a car drive across the gravel. I recognize the sound it makes. It's Daddy. He's come back. Al and I run out of the kitchen, through the entrance hall. We press our faces against the glass panes of the front door. The grownups hurry after us.

"I must say he knows how to dress," Juliet says, peering over us. Daddy's wearing a green jacket the same color as his car. A gold handkerchief sticks out the breast pocket.

"I wonder what he wants," Ethel says.

"I'll go and see," Mummy says, glancing in the mirror. "Oh dear, I didn't put on any lipstick."

I move to follow Mummy, but Juliet places her hand on my shoulder.

We watch Mummy walk slowly over to Daddy. She shades her eyes with one hand to look up at him. Daddy says, "I need to talk to you." I didn't hear him say that, but I could see his lips. I'm not as good a lipreader as Al, but I can understand certain things. He says something very fast, switching to French. He glances over at us. Juliet says she mustn't forget her bacon and Ethel follows her.

Mummy and Daddy turn so that their backs are to us. Their shadows are in front. They walk a little ways across the gravel yard and stand beside the blood-red roses which line the side of the river. They talk and talk but we can't hear or see what they're saying. We just watch them shake their heads or move their hands. Then Daddy leans over Mummy and places his hand on her shoulder and she moves back a step. He lets his arm drop, then brushes his hand through his hair and shrugs his shoulders. He points to his car. She shakes her head.

"Come and have your breakfast," Juliet shouts from the kitchen.

Now Daddy is facing us. I ask Al to translate.

She says Dad asked Mum to go for a drive with him.

He says he'll drive slowly. He'll drive like Luis if she likes. He says that it's hard to talk like this.

Suddenly, Mummy rushes towards the car and opens the passenger's door and gets in.

Daddy walks over to the other side and the car starts up. They drive through the white gate and up the road, disappearing over the hill.

I wish they had taken us.

I stare at the gravel and at Mme Daudiet's cottage. When it's sunny, the glass windows reflect the blue sky and when it's gray the windows are blank.

"I wonder if we should turn on a light," Ethel says again, as I wander back into the kitchen.

Granny pulls out another piece from inside her brioche.

I sit down and separate my eggs into three piles.

"What did I say?" Ethel says. "Didn't I warn you?"

"Yes, yes," Granny says. "You've already pointed that out. But it doesn't hurt to be optimistic."

I pass some egg down to Max who is lying under the table. His tongue feels warm against my palm.

"I keep forgetting to eat those prunes," Ethel says.

"Ethel is constipated," I say.

"Really," Ethel says. "You needn't advertise it to the world."

I watch Ethel eat her prunes. She puts one in her mouth and then she slowly moves it round just like she does with her mint, then she puts her hand in front of her mouth and spits her pit into her hand before hiding it in a paper napkin. She keeps pushing prunes across the kitchen table to Granny, but Granny keeps pushing them back.

After breakfast, Juliet says she's going to open her packet. Every month Juliet's friend Nancy sends her English magazines. Juliet says she likes to keep abreast of who is marrying who and who is having an affair with whom among English royalty. She likes to show us pictures of their houses and country estates. I follow Juliet and Al, counting the number of steps to her room. Twenty-three. I watch Al open the packet, very carefully, without tearing the paper because she knows that Juliet wants to keep it. Juliet always saves brown paper or wrapping paper.

I wander over to the card table with Juliet's puzzle. She's only done a few more pieces. Now what looked like the bottom of a pale green boat has a pink flower drawn across it.

I lie on my stomach over the red poof and pretend to read one of the magazines. I ask Juliet if it often happens that someone has an affair and then gets back together with their wife.

"All the time," she says. "Particularly in France. Why, there'd hardly be any married people left if they didn't. Ninety percent of French couples have been unfaithful to one another. Of course, in England it's quite different."

"I'm not going to have an affair when I get married," I say.

"That's good," Juliet says, and laughs.

"I'm not going to get married," Al says.

"Well, girls, now that you've decided all that how about helping me look for travel articles?"

Besides articles on English royalty, Juliet likes to collect articles on exotic places. She keeps them in a red folder with a white label that says _Holidays._ Today we find three articles: one on Corfu, another on Corsica, and another on the Lake District of England. Juliet says she's not sure whether to include the Lake District because the weather is bound to be as it is everywhere else in England.

"Daddy says the food in England is terrible," I say.

"There are some very good dishes."

"Like what?" I ask.

"Like Yorkshire pudding," she says.

I think I hear a car and I rush to the window but there's no one.

"Speaking of food reminds me of my diet," Juliet says. "I have drawn up a whole new chart with the number of calories I'm allowed each day. This is a carbohydrate diet. I can't eat anything but carbohydrates."

She pulls out the top drawer of her chest.

I notice the dahlias in a vase on top of her chest.

"I know your secret," I lipsing to Al.

She smiles.

"Who gave you the flowers?" I ask Juliet.

"Never you mind."

"I know," I say.

She shows me a white piece of paper across which she has drawn lines, dividing it into boxes, with a date for each box and a blank for her to write the number of calories.

"Can I go on a diet?" I ask.

"Me too?" Al asks.

"Of course not. You're both as thin as rails. I have been wondering if the scale out here in the country isn't a little over, just by a pound or two."

"When are they coming back?" I ask Juliet.

"I don't know."

"I wish they'd come soon," I say.

"Maybe they'll both run away," Al says.

"That seems unlikely," Juliet says.

***

It's late afternoon now. The shadows are long. The grass almost blue. We're playing un, deux, trois, soleil. It was Al's idea so she's the one standing with her back to us. All the grownups are playing, even Ethel and Juliet and Luis. Al says un, deux, trois, very slowly and then soleil very fast as she swings round.

"Gabriel," she says. " I saw you."

"It's not fair," I say. "She keeps cheating." If she hadn't cheated, I would have reached her a long time ago. Juliet looks very funny standing on one foot, trying to balance herself. Ethel is so cautious she's only advanced a few steps. Granny has almost reached Al. She's only a few feet away, but she seems to be taking an awfully long time to get up to Al.

When she does touch Al's shoulder, she says she's a little tired, would I like to take her place, but then Ethel says she's had enough and Juliet says she should get ready for her evening out so I don't get a turn.

91

Al and I lie on the grass by Granny and Ethel's feet.

"It's almost dinner time," Ethel says.

"Not quite," Granny says. "It's not even six."

"What shall we have for dinner?" Ethel says. "I don't think there's much. Some cold lamb perhaps."

"Cold lamb will do fine," Granny says.

Then we see Mummy. She stands in the doorway of the kitchen.

We all rush over. "Where's Daddy?" I ask.

"He's gone."

"How come we didn't get to see him?" Al asks.

"I'm sorry, girls. We had to talk and it took us much longer than we thought but you will get to see him soon. I promise. Another time."

I can't tell if Mummy had a good time or not with Daddy.

"Darlings," Mummy says. "I have to get changed. I have another date with the doctor."

"Tonight?" Ethel asks.

"He should be here any minute," Mummy says.

"My goodness," Ethel says. "What would we have done if you—"

"I know. I know. It would have been very awkward. That's why I had him drop me off at Estouy. I walked from there."

***

The moon looks just like a popped boiled egg. Al and I stare at it from our window. I think I can see the earth reflected. The river is loud today. It's like a person. Sometimes, it talks a lot and on other days not at all. "Let's walk through the garden," Al says. She climbs out the window first. We could go down the back stairs but it's more fun this way. We swing down from the ledge, rest our feet on top of one of the green shutters of the bathroom downstairs, then lower ourselves onto the bathroom ledge. We jump onto the small bridge that's just outside the window.

Mist rises from the grass, hiding most of the trees. Now and again a white flower stands out. We don't notice Luis's car in the middle of the gravel until we're only a few feet away. Then we stop.

The car looks almost gray in this light. Juliet and Luis are smoking so that it seems as if the mist has slipped inside their car. There's something funny about them. It's because Luis is sitting in the back seat with Juliet. Juliet looks straight over at me. I expect her to say something, but she doesn't. It's as if I'm invisible. Perhaps she does not see me, I think, because she isn't wearing her glasses. Al and I slip back into the house, using the stairs this time. We lie in bed next to one another, waiting to hear Juliet come into her room.

Ten

Voices, a muffled laugh, followed by a bark drift up to my room.

"I don't know if that's a compliment," I hear the doctor say.

"I mean it as a compliment," Mummy says.

I pull the sheets and blanket over my head.

"It's time we wrote Mummy's date in the calendar," Al says, pulling at the sheet.

"I don't feel like it," I say.

I hear her footsteps as she goes into Juliet's room and takes down the calendar that is hanging over her bed. Al always gets the calendar because she won't get into as much trouble if Juliet wakes. She presents the calendar and a pen to me and I circle the date and write in as small as I can the number five. Mummy has been on five dates with the doctor. We fight over whether this morning should count as a new date since Mum didn't come back last night. We decide to wait and see if they spend the whole day together.

We tiptoe back to Juliet's room. Al's about to hang the calendar up, when Juliet sits up in her bed and says, "What do you think you're doing?" Al says she wanted to see the calendar.

"You don't need to take it down to do that. Here, pass it to me. I'll put it back up. My goodness! How time flies. We've been here almost a month."

"I think it's been going very slowly," I say.

"That's because you're so young. Wait until you're my age. A year seems like a day."

"But you were the one who was ticking off the days," I say; then I remember how Mum said that the days go by so fast when you're in love.

"Juliet's in love," I say.

"Don't be ridiculous," she says.

"Juliet's in love," Al says and jumps up on Juliet's bed.

Juliet tells her to get off immediately.

"Juliet's in love," Al and I shout together.

"I'm not the one in love," she says, tearing off pages from her calendar.

I wonder if she is thinking of Mummy.

"We missed the portrait of Queen Elizabeth the Second," Juliet says.

She shows it to us. I'm always disappointed with portraits of the queen because she never looks the way I picture a queen. She reminds me of Juliet.

"Juliet, I think you look like Queen Elizabeth."

"Me," she says, pointing to her chest. "Me. What a funny idea—"

"You do."

"Then you should treat me with a little more respect," she says.

I lean out her window and stare at the river. I'm too high up to see fish.

"It's so boring here," I say. "What are we going to do today?"

"You can help me with my puzzle. You can work on your tree-houses. Clean up your rooms."

"Oh no, Juliet." I walk out of her room and down the stairs. I try to tiptoe through the living room without Mummy and the doctor seeing me.

"Gabriel," Mummy says. "You're up early. Come and say hello to Xavier." Mummy is sitting on the couch in the cream dress she wore on her first date. She is pulling one of the pearl buttons on her shirt. It makes me think of Daddy who used to place his hand over Mummy's hands when she fidgeted at table.

The doctor sits with his legs together, hands resting on his knees.

I try to walk on the bright side of the rug, but to reach the doctor I have to step in the part that has been faded by the sun. Even when I shake hands with him, I do not look up. I stare at the tips of his shoes. They're an ugly red-brown color and they've got mud on the edges.

"Good morning," I say.

"Good morning," he says.

I turn to go.

"Don't go away," Mummy says. "Come and talk to us."

I sit next to my mother on the couch and stare at the painting of the sailboat hanging above the chest of drawers. Juliet dusted the painting yesterday, and now it's lopsided, tilting slightly to the left, and just above one sail she left a patch of dust that hovers like a cloud above the ship.

"What are you going to do today?" Mummy asks.

"I don't know. It's so boring here."

"I've never heard you say that before," Mummy says.

The doctor leans forward and his hair catches the light. His eyes are blue.

"I think I saw you the other day. A red canoe."

"No, ours is orange," I say.

"It might have been orange," he says.

"Xavier loves to sail. He's originally from Brittany. You know where that is?"

"Yes," I say.

"You should be careful not to go further than the green bridge," he says. "After that there are dams."

"Do you have to cut up lots of dead people every day?" I ask.

"No, just now and then." He laughs.

Mummy says, "Really, Gabriel, the questions you ask."

"Can I go now?"

"Of course, darling."

"I've got lots of work to do on my treehouse."

"We'll come by in a little while and you can show us," Mummy says.

All morning we work on our trees, and the sun gets hotter and hotter and the grass smells as if it's about to burn and the sky is so blue it hurts your eyes to look at it. I keep glancing over my shoulder at the house, expecting to see the doctor and Mummy step out of the front door or walk along the bank, but all I see is Max sniffing and a moor hen, flapping its wings trying to get away from him.

It gets so hot that Al and I sit on the edge of the bank with our legs dangling in the river. We watch blue dragonflies glide across the river and sometimes we see a white or yellow butterfly.

"Did you see Daddy again?" Al asks.

"No," I say. "But I found out something about the doctor."

"What?"

"I can't tell you because you always give my secrets away."

"I promise I won't this time," she says.

"Cross your heart and hope to die."

She slowly crosses her heart.

"The doctor kidnaps babies."

"Where does he hide them?" she asks.

"Behind a thick velour curtain," I say.

"How do you know?" she asks.

"I heard them when Mummy and I went over to his house the other day." I imitate their cries. "Hu. Haa."

"You think he'll kidnap us?" Al asks.

"Oh no, we're too old."

"Even me?"

"Yes," I say. "Come on. Let's go for a swim."

We pull off our clothes and climb up a tree. We swing down from a slim branch and drop into the river. We shout and scream, but no one comes. Holding hands, we let ourselves drift down the river on our backs. Sometimes we feel weeds brush against our legs and we screech.

We stand outside on the wooden bridge, peering through the water lily curtains at Mummy and the doctor sitting on Granny's couch. Mummy is laughing. Her laughter goes higher and higher until it seems like it can't go any higher, and then her laugh trails off and we hear his laugh, a deep laugh. We continue to stare at the back of their heads and perhaps I stare too hard because the doctor turns round. He smiles but we run away. We tiptoe upstairs to Juliet's room. She's gone into town with Granny and Aunt Ethel. We take turns sitting on her red poof. We pull at the green wallpaper and stare at her puzzle, adding a few pieces. Al and I were both wrong. The puzzle isn't of boats or flowers. It's of a pale green teapot with a pink flower drawn on one side. I tell Al about the red box with the cards and photographs. We peer under her bed but there are just bottles and we line them up on the window sill. She has several of the same kind. A man with a red jacket and white pants. He looks just like the soldiers who stand in front of the Queen of England's Palace.

I pull on Juliet's red high-heeled shoes. They're hard to walk in. It feels like I'm on stilts. I try on her black satin dress. I don't have any boobs so I stuff into the bodice a pair of her panties instead. We get the giggles. Al pulls on Juliet's dress with the airplanes. The hem touches the floor. She wears Juliet's black high heels. Slowly, holding hands, we glide-hobble across the floor pretending we're going to be presented to the queen. We go through all Juliet's clothes except for her wig. Through the floor boards I can hear opera. Al says she can feel the vibrations through her feet.

We make up a pretend restaurant. I get to be Juliet. Al has to be the waiter. She comes by and pours some wine. I pick up my glass with my pinky sticking out and I say, "A bit dry but it will do," and we get the giggles again. Then we switch and I'm the waiter and get to drop the cheese soufflé down Juliet's dress and Al screams. She screams so loudly that Mummy comes running upstairs. We run out onto the landing so that she doesn't come inside Juliet's room. She doesn't notice how we're dressed.

"What's the matter?" she says.

"Nothing," I say. "We're just playing."

"We're going to have lunch in a minute," she says. "Granny and Aunt Ethel must be running late."

We're waiting in the dining room. The doctor is sitting at the head of the table in Daddy's place. He's staring at his glass, running one finger along the rim. The whistle becomes louder and louder. Al wets her finger and runs it along the rim of her glass. She says she can feel the sound squeak through her finger and then I do too and soon there are three whistles competing to be the loudest and drown out the other two.

We stop only when we hear the sound of a car driving across the gravel. I imagine that it's my father's car even though it doesn't sound like his. I picture my father swinging open the door to his green Porsche, striding across the gravel, his head going from side to side. "Get out," he tells Xavier.

But it isn't my father. It's Granny and Aunt Ethel and Juliet.

We watch them through the glass door of the entrance.

"I'm so sorry we're late, darling," Granny says. "But would you believe it? I bought all these beads and wool and forgot them at the doctor's so we had to drive all the way back."

"But the doctor's here," I say.

"Oh no," Granny says. "This was a specialist. A friend of our doctor's. Very nice."

"Is everything all right?" Mummy asks.

"I think so," Granny says.

"Oh good," Mummy says. "Well, everything's ready. We're just

98

having pâté and bread and some salad. There's a little foie gras and of course cheese. The doctor is here. Girls, why don't you run in and keep him company while I bring it in?"

The doctor now stands staring out the window which looks onto the garden. He doesn't turn when we come in so Al and I pull out our chairs and sit down. Then he starts sneezing. He sneezes and sneezes. "Merde," he says. If Juliet heard me say that she'd hit my head.

"Xavier suffers from hay fever just like your mother," Mummy says, as she enters the dining room. "Maybe that's why you don't like flowers."

"No," he says. "It's because I associate flowers with funerals. When I was a boy I was forced to go to a funeral. I don't believe children should have to go to them."

"Maybe you're right," Mummy says. "They are very upsetting."

"I've never been to a funeral," I say.

"I haven't either," Al says.

"Let's hope you don't for a long time," Mummy says.

Granny and Ethel come into the dining room. They've put on fresh lipstick and combed their hair.

"How is your foot today?" the doctor asks Granny.

"Completely better. Almost ready to do a Scottish jig."

"A jig?" the doctor asks.

"A dance," Mummy says.

"Please, please, please, will you do one, Granny?" Al asks.

"I was just joking," Granny answers.

"Juliet can do a Scottish jig," Al says, as Juliet comes into the dining room. She's changed into her favorite dress with the airplanes. She's also put on lipstick except hers is brown. I expect her to say something about her room; we didn't have time to clean it up. But all she says is, "I don't know what you're talking about."

"Yes, you do," Al says.

I kick Al under the table but she doesn't understand. I'm afraid to lipsing.

"I'm ravenous," Mummy says. "Do sit down, everyone."

At first, everyone concentrates on eating. The doctor holds his knife funny like he's going to stab someone. Juliet won't approve. I mouth to Al that he holds his knife funny. She laughs and Juliet glances over at me. I know what that look means.

"Have you lived here long?" Aunt Ethel asks.

"About ten years. Before that we lived in Etampes."

"Your wife—"

"We're divorced."

"I'm so sorry," Ethel says.

"It was for the best."

"My husband died a year after we married," Ethel says. "We lived on a farm miles and miles from anywhere. I continued to live there several years afterwards but then it got too hard—"

I remember visiting Ethel's farm. There were cloth frogs filled with beans all over her house. Hundreds and hundreds of them. She gave me one and I made a hole and let all the beans out. Now it's flat. She also had amethyst stones everywhere. I stole a dark purple one from her mantelpiece. I had to climb on a chair to get it.

Ethel talks a lot to the doctor. She tells him how her husband was a doctor, only a real doctor. The doctor and Mummy smile when she says that. Granny laughs. Juliet tells him about how she used to be a nurse during the Second World War and how hard the doctors had to work in those days. She explains to the doctor that she likes being a nanny better because that way you get to travel.

My Daddy gets to travel a lot. Once he went to India where vultures swoop down and take your food while you eat.

Granny asks the doctor about his family. He says that he has a twin. I try to imagine someone just like him, but then he says that his twin is not identical. She's a girl and she looks completely different. Granny says she had a twin and everyone looks surprised, even Aunt Ethel.

"Really, mother?" Mummy says. "You never told me that."

"He died when I was still a baby," Granny says. "I have no memory of him."

After the doctor leaves, the grownups sit around the living room having their coffee, saying how nice he is. Mummy says that everyone confides in him because he is a psychiatrist and used to listening to other people. I expect Juliet to give us a talking-to but she doesn't. I mouth to Al: "Boring. Boring. Boring". We march around the house pretending to be soldiers. We shout the French anthem at the top of our lungs. Alons enfants de la patrie. Le jour de gloire est arrivé. Juliet gets really mad. She hates it when we sing, particularly the French anthem. But it's much better than the English, I say, and that gets her even madder. Still she doesn't say anything about her room. She makes us lie down on our beds but I can't sleep. Al does almost immediately. I know because she breathes louder.

I wait until everything is quiet and then I wander from room to room, brushing the palm of one hand along the cool walls. Granny's sleeping with Tiger on top of her head. Mummy's not in her bedroom. I wonder if she's gone to see the doctor. Max sleeps on her bed, his head hanging sadly over the side. I lie down beside him and stroke his soft ears. Poor Max, I say, you've been punished. If you hadn't been naughty they wouldn't have left you behind. Did you steal more chickens? He does not answer and I stop talking to him and listen to the wind making the curtain hangers rattle.

I walk over to the closet and finger Mummy's dresses. I wonder what happened to the suitcase with Daddy's clothes. I remember how Mummy would always have us check Daddy's suit pockets when she ran out of money. I look under her bed but there's nothing. Just a ball of dust and a blue marble.

I think I can hear someone singing and then I realize it's coming from the other side of the house. It's Juliet. By the time I reach her room, though, she's stopped. I can't believe it. Juliet's tidied up her room completely. Her books are all in the shelves, the top of her chest of drawers gleams. She's even got fresh roses in a vase. Her bed is made with the corners tucked in like hospital corners. Sitting in her green armchair, she is wearing a new dress with white circles that look like buoys. She does not notice me staring at her. She's concentrating on a new Agatha Christie and she's done her nails a different color: pale pink.

Eleven

"Juliet," I say, shaking her by her shoulders as hard as I can. "Juliet, she's gone."

"Stop," Juliet says, rolling onto her back, staring at me from tiny swollen red eyes, her pink nylon nightdress twisted around her waist, showing her white panties. "You're bruising me. What is the matter? You are always waking me at some ungodly hour. Who's gone?"

"Mummy," I say.

"Don't be ridiculous," she says, sitting up and glancing at her clock, a little red one with a speckled face. "It's later than I thought. She's probably just gone for a walk or to buy some fresh eggs and milk."

"No, no. She didn't take Max and she's not with the doctor. She took her car."

"Well, I'm sure there's some logical explanation we haven't thought of," she says.

She stretches and teases her hair with her fingers. I cross my arms over my chest because it's always cold in Juliet's room.

I follow her into the bathroom. She brushes her teeth, then her tongue. She says it's very important in order to have good breath. She also sprays her mouth with mint.

"What a lot of laundry I have to do!" Juliet exclaims as she peers into the basket with our dirty clothes. She pulls out one of my dresses and examines it. "This looks perfectly clean. You're very naughty, Gabriel. You just throw your clothes into the bin because it's easier than hanging them up or folding them. I'm not going to put up with it."

She sits down at her table and does a few puzzle pieces. It's not just a picture of a teapot with shadows. There are also matching tea cups that look like they're about to march off the table. I like the green felt that covers the table and pass my hand over it.

The telephone rings and I run downstairs. It's Daddy.

"Hello?" he says.

"Hello," I whisper.

"Hello? Is that you, Gabriel? I can't hear you. Speak up."

"It's me," I say, playing with the telephone cord. It's very long and I wind it round and round my arm.

"How are you?"

"Fine." I'm still whispering but I can't help it. I can hear my voice trembling a bit. I've wound the telephone cord so tight it hurts.

"Is your mother there?"

"No."

"Do you know where she is?"

"No, but Juliet says she's bound to be back soon." I tug at the phone cord but I'm afraid I'll unplug it.

"She was supposed to meet me over an hour ago."

"Maybe she got lost."

"Maybe—"

"Maybe she's run into a lot of traffic."

"Maybe," he says.

"I saw you."

"When? I'm sorry I didn't get to talk to you when I came the other day."

"No, I saw you before that in the wild field."

"That wasn't me."

"It was," I say.

"It wasn't," he says.

"It was," I say.

"It wasn't," he says.

I can feel my cheeks getting hotter.

"Where's your sense of humor?" Daddy says. "I promise it wasn't me. Look, I have to go now, but I'll see you soon. Remember, your daddy loves you. Bye."

Slowly I unwind my arm from the cord. It's easy now that I don't have my ear pressed against the receiver. His voice sounded far away. But he can't be in Brussels. Brussels is too far away for Mummy to meet him.

Through the glass door, I stare at the gravel yard. The stones glint. The roses along the river are a deep red. Granny and I have not gone to see the roses along the white fence for a long time. I tip-toe through the living room, past Granny's room where I can see

103

Ethel seated in a chair by Granny's bed. Ethel does not read or knit. She just sits. Sometimes she folds back the corner of her bed jacket and irons it with one hand then she unfolds it. Granny has been sleeping later and later.

Upstairs Juliet is still working on her puzzle.

"Was that your mother on the phone?" She asks, one puzzle piece between her teeth.

"No," I say. "It was Daddy."

She places the puzzle piece and then Al appears in the doorway. "How come no one woke me up?"

Juliet fits another piece.

"Stop," Al says. "It's my turn."

I walk over to Juliet's window. I lean out and stare at the water. It's gray when the clouds cover the sun. I catch sight of muskrats just as they disappear beneath the house.

The doctor is walking across the gravel. He's wearing jeans and a white T-shirt. He knocks on the front door and looks up. I quickly pull in my head.

"What was that?" Juliet says.

"It's the doctor," I say.

"Come on," she says.

Juliet marches downstairs. Al and I walk slowly down the steps, holding onto the red velour cord. Then we go up the stairs again and sit halfway. We rest our elbows on our knees, our chins in our hands, and we stare out the window which is smudged from our fingers.

"I daresay she'll be back soon," I hear Ethel say.

"Probably gone for a drive," Juliet says.

"Do have a seat," Ethel says.

"I'll make coffee, or would you prefer tea?" Juliet asks.

"No, no, I don't want to put you to any trouble."

"No trouble at all," Juliet says. "You sit over there."

When Al and I wander into the living room, the doctor is sitting in the blue and white striped chair. "Hello," he says, standing up and then sitting down.

Granny and Aunt Ethel are knitting. Juliet's sitting in the big yellow armchair. They've all moved their chairs over to the doctor's so that they can hear him because he talks so softly. The doctor tells them about a patient who bit a piece out of his cheek.

"Oh no," Ethel says. I stare at his cheek, but I can't see any mark.

Ethel complains that she could not get a wink of sleep because of the toilet running all night. Granny says she thought it was the sound of the river running. The doctor offers to fix it. "Oh no," Ethel says. "No, no, no." The doctor insists.

Everyone except for Granny follows him into the bathroom. It's very crowded because the bathroom is not very big and because there are so many of us. The doctor rolls up his sleeves, lifts the top off the tank, and reaches inside. "Ooh," Ethel says. "Don't you want a pair of gloves?"

"No, no, I'll just wash my hands afterwards," he answers.

Al and I both want to peer inside the tank.

"Does anyone have an elastic?" He asks. "I'm going to have to do something temporary. We need to replace the—"

Juliet runs upstairs. She brings the doctor a pink elastic of mine.

"This ought to work," he says, after fiddling inside the tank, replacing the top. We all watch him flush the toilet, then wait to see if there's any noise afterwards. There's only the sound of the river.

"Fancy that? A handyman as well as a doctor," Ethel says. She smiles up at the doctor and she places one hand on his arm. Ethel's husband was a very good handyman too. He built her a beautiful oak bed. She had to leave it behind on the farm because it was too big for the room at Granny's.

I lipsing to Al that Ethel's in love with the doctor. Ethel's in love with the doctor. Al laughs and hugs herself, pretending to give kisses. Then she says why don't we go play in our treehouses, but Juliet says we can't go play outside because it's about to storm, so we play with our dolls beneath the stairs of the living room. We pretend that the small dolls are aristocrats and about to be guillotined by the big dolls. We use the boy dolls for the executioners. We have each doll lie with their neck bare and then bang, we cut off their heads. I get to pretend to be Marie Antoinette who moans and groans because she has no pastries to eat.

The doctor talks and talks about how they need to reform hospitals for mental patients. It gets darker and darker until Juliet gets up and switches on a lamp. Lightening strikes and the lamp flickers out.

"I do hope she's not out in this weather," Ethel remarks.

"If she's in the car, there's nothing to worry about," Juliet says.

"She's always liked the rain," Granny says. "Even as a little girl she would run out into the garden."

Suddenly, the front door slams shut. Mummy stands in the doorway with her clothes stuck to her body. Her hair has come undone. She looks upset.

We stare at her. I can't tell if she's seen Daddy. Everyone starts talking at once.

"Are you—" Granny says.

"Soaked through," Ethel says.

"Take a hot bath," Juliet says.

Al and I run over to Mummy and put our arms around her. She smells of the rain. She kisses us everywhere: on the top of our heads, on our cheeks, on our necks. She stops only when the doctor says, "We were so worried." She looks up and says, "I'm sorry. I didn't mean to worry anyone."

"Better get changed before you catch your death," Ethel says.

"Yes," Juliet says. "Nothing like a wet head."

We watch Mummy run upstairs, then there's the sound of water. She must be taking a hot bath. Ethel and Granny go back to their knitting, but Al and I don't feel like playing dolls anymore. We just sit on the couch and lift our legs and let them drop, banging the side of the couch, until Juliet tells us to stop.

The doctor wanders over to the window and stares out. He opens his wallet. Al says he has a photograph of Mum he's always looking at. I wonder if he knows that Mum went to see Dad.

When Mummy comes downstairs in her beige skirt and a white shirt, she sits between Al and me.

"Not a nice day," Ethel says.

"No, it isn't," Granny says.

"Just dreadful," Juliet says.

The doctor looks down at his trousers, then stands. "I suppose I should go." Mummy stands up. He walks a few steps towards the entrance hall but Mummy stops him.

"I need to talk to you," she says.

Granny says it's way past her forty winks even though it's the morning. Ethel says that she's been meaning to write a postcard to her daughter Heather for weeks. Juliet says we must go for a walk.

"It's not raining anymore," she says. "It's just sprinkling. A bit of fresh air will do you good. Hurry and don't argue with me." She charges out the living room, holding each of us by the hand.

We have to pass Mummy and the doctor in the entrance hall on our way to the bathroom where we keep our boots. They stand opposite each other and the rain from the glass door is reflected on their faces and clothes.

"I'm sorry," we hear Mummy say. "I'm so sorry. I'm just so confused. The worse is that I'm beginning to sound like him. That's what he would always say to me. I can't help it if I'm in love with two people at the same time—"

"Marry me," he says.

"Don't be silly," she says. "I barely know you. I'm not divorced."

Juliet bangs the closet doors closed. She pulls on her square-toed red gumboots and her yellow raincoat and matching hat. She walks very fast out of the house, across the gravel yard, through the gate and along the white fence with the roses. We have to run to keep up with her. She slows down only when we reach the first green bridge. "Ah," she says. "I feel better already."

The air is so moist it feels as if we've been dipped in water, and the countryside so still and silent our footsteps echo; and as we walk along the road the river appears and disappears beneath the mist. The sky darkens. At first it's white, but then it turns gray, then charcoal. The smell of wet earth is very strong. Juliet tells us how when she was a girl she and her brothers moved from London and lived in the country in a house that was next to a bakery. They did not have to leave the house to reach the bakery. They could go down through the basement. Her brothers liked to hit mice that jumped out of bags of flour. Once her brothers gave her a fright by offering her a box with a dead mouse wrapped in cotton wool. I don't listen to Juliet. I imagine my mother's wedding instead. She's dressed in white with a long veil that reaches the ground and she's carrying muguet. The doctor walks with tiny quick steps up the aisle. He's wearing a tight gray suit. I imagine the minister asking the congregation whether anyone knows of any reason whether these two people should not be joined in holy matrimony. My father steps forward. He's wearing Mummy's favorite shirt of his, the blue one, the same color as the swallows.

On the last stretch back along a muddy unpaved road, the sky is almost black and we keep tripping in our mud-caked boots. We would fall if we weren't holding each other's hands. When the house comes into sight, we don't have the strength to run. We stare at the light spilling out of each window onto the ivy leaves. I search for a green Porsche in the shadows.

***

The light is on in Granny's room. Tiger sits beneath the lamp. Every few minutes she jerks her head out because it gets too hot. Granny's sitting on the water-lily couch reading her book. She's almost finished it. "Do you want to hear the rest?" she asks, placing her bookmark inside her book and closing it.

"No," I say. "They all finish the same."

"I thought you liked that," Granny says.

"I don't," I say.

"That's because you're getting so grown up. Soon you'll be reading books like your mother's."

I walk over to her window and stare at the garden. It looks like nighttime even though it's only three o'clock. All the trees are dripping water and the roses outside Granny's bedroom window droop.

I don't hear Granny get up from the couch. She has the softest footsteps. Often she gives Ethel a fright. Suddenly, she's beside me.

"Look at the leaves of that tree," she says.

She places her hand on my shoulder.

"Aren't they beautiful? They're all back to front and almost silver in this light. And look at the drops of water in that cobweb."

"I don't like spiders," I say.

"They're very useful, you know. They kill mosquitoes and flies and other nuisances," she says.

"May I ask you a question, Granny?"

"Of course."

"Do you think Mummy'll marry the doctor?"

"I don't know."

"I thought you knew everything."

"Of course not," Granny says. "Whatever gave you that idea? I'm very ignorant about many, many things. But I wouldn't worry about it. They've only known each other a few weeks. It's a bit premature—"

She leans out the window and reaches for a yellow rose brushed with pink. It falls apart in her hand.

"Would you like to put on some music and do a little ballet?" Granny asks. "I'd love to see the new steps you've learned this year."

"No," I say. "I don't feel like it."

"Well," Granny says. "How would you like to just sit next to me and tell me what you would like to do most?"

"I'd like to go with you on the QEII," I say. "I wish we didn't have to wait until I'm sixteen."

"Maybe we don't," Granny says. "Maybe the two of us could go next year."

"I wish I could go with you when you go back to South Africa," I say. "I wish you didn't have to go."

"I wish I didn't too," Granny says. "But we still have almost three weeks."

"Tell me all about the QEII," I say. "I want to know every single thing."

"Well, let me see. There are tables that are screwed to the floor so that they don't drift across when the sea is rough—"

Twelve

It's morning, but the sun has not yet reached the wood armoire in Granny's room; the carved rose and the bird are still in the shadows. The house is still.

I walk upstairs to my room where Al is asleep with her monkey without its head resting in her arms. She holds her white blanket with the blue flowers pressed to her nose. I think of pressing her blanket to my nose, but I know it won't make me feel better anymore.

Juliet's sleeping in her pink see-through nightdress. Her room is still neat. She has even put out on the armchair the clothes she plans to wear: her pantyhose and her cream bra and underwear, a red and green dress. I lift her bra from the chair and wonder what it would be like to have breasts that big, but then Juliet twitches in her sleep and I run down the stairs as fast as I can. I sit on the couch and stare at the grandfather clock. I imagine that the boat is floating across its face. Daddy loves watches. He owns a watch that tells the position of the sun and moon.

Granny appears in her nightdress in the doorway of her room. "I was thinking we should see the roses today," she says. "I'll just pull on my dressing gown."

"Okay," I say.

I hold Granny's arm while she bends over and pulls on her white slippers with the white powder puffs.

I pull on Juliet's red gumboots.

As soon as we step out the front door, Granny breathes in deeply and says, "Smell that sweet air!" The grass is wet. It's very green from all the rain and it's grown so high it reaches my knees. The mist is even thicker than usual. We do not talk. I know that Granny is listening for larks. I drag my feet. Juliet's boots are too big and chafe my heels. Now and then I kick the white fence, watching paint fall off in flakes. "Sh," Granny says.

The hedges are still; not one branch quivers, only the mist shifts, but then the sun pierces through the mist streaking the lawn and we see a lark. It rises steeply above the mist, its tail outspread. It flies higher and higher; it's motionless, as if suspended high above us and now it slowly glides down, wings extended. It glides down and down then suddenly closes its wings and plummets, opening its wings at the very last second before touching the ground.

Granny says, "Now, isn't that wonderful?" and I say, "It's okay."

"Just think—if I hadn't got out of bed we would have missed it," she says. "And look at those roses!"

There are so many roses it looks as if the fence might collapse beneath their weight. I've never seen so many before. Granny cuts a few roses from each rosebush and places them in a special basket that's made for flowers.

"What are you wearing those for?" Granny asks, pointing to my red gum boots.

"I don't know. They're Juliet's."

"But you usually go barefooted."

"I don't like it anymore," I say.

Granny cuts a few roses.

"It was just like that for me with the skin of milk," Granny says.

"You liked it?"

"Well, it didn't bother me and then I couldn't stand it. I remember Ethel used to tease me and eat hers slowly in front of me and I'd beg her not to because just seeing her eat it made me feel ill."

The tops of the trees are turning gold. A sliver of sun appears. The river runs in and out of bands of mist.

"Granny, do you think Daddy will come back?"

"I don't know," she says.

"He might," I say.

"It's possible," she says.

She raises her hand and her bracelets jingle but I move before her hand touches my head.

I do one cartwheel after the next along the white fence. Granny claps her hands when I'm finished.

"Why did you clap?" I ask. "They weren't any good."

"Yes, they were. Good enough for me."

I race back to the house without looking over my shoulder.

Mummy stands in the entrance hall in front of the mirror arranging a vase of the roses Granny and I cut this morning. She pulls one from the back and tucks it in front. She pulls out another, then stands holding the flower as if she's forgotten what she meant to do with it. Her face takes on a dreamy look. "He recites so beautifully," she says.   "Ainsi toujours poussés vers de nouveaux rivages, Dans la nuit éternelle emportés sans retour, Ne pourrons-nous jamais sur l'océan des ages jeter l'ancre un seul jour?"

She stops when she sees my reflection in the mirror.

"How are you, darling. Isn't it a beautiful day?"

"It's okay."

"Guess what?" she says.

"What?"

"Xavier's invited us over for dinner."

"Great," I say.

"Don't you like him?" she asks.

"He's okay."

"He's really a very sweet man. He adores children. You'll see, when you get to know him—"

"Do I have to go?" I ask.

"I'd be very disappointed if you didn't," she says.

I run out into the garden over the wood bridges, past the silver willows. I see Al.

"Hey, what are you doing in my tree?"

"I've got all these things," she says. "Come see."

"Mummy says we have to have dinner with the doctor tonight."

"I know. He's going to make pommes frites."

Pommes frites are Al's favorite dish.

"They're going to celebrate their three-week anniversary since they met," she says.

I climb up into my tree. There's a rug and an old crocheted blanket across the bunk bed. Pots and pans hang from branches. We're saving special teacups for when the queen of England comes to visit. They're white with a purple border and they look like they're made of mother of pearl. We lower a red bucket into the river, then pull it back up. We fill our cups with water and pretend to drink tea.

"Let's play the pretend game," I say. "You be the doctor and I'll be Mummy and Daddy."

"That's not fair," Al says. "You can't be Mummy and Daddy. I want to be them."

"Well, you can't because I chose first," I say.

"I won't play," she says.

"Spoilsport," I say.

"You're a spoilsport," she says.

"All right, you can be Daddy and the doctor and I'll be Mummy. I've got long hair so I should play Mummy."

"Then can we exchange?"

"Okay." I sit down on the bunkbed and put my two dolls beside me. "Once upon a time," I say.

"I'm hungry. Can we eat?" I have one doll say.

"No darling," I say. "We have to wait for Daddy."

"Is he coming soon?" I have the other doll say.

"I don't know, darling. I hope so."

"I'm getting tired," Al says. "You're doing all the talking."

"Well, you can't come yet. The father comes late."

"I want to come now. I'm sick of waiting. Hello, darling," Al says, leaning over and pulling up imaginary pants. "Load of shit work at the office."

"That's not what he says. He says he had a shit load of work at the office," I say.

"Okay. Okay. A shit load of work," she says.

"I'm afraid the roast beef is completely overcooked," I say.

"I'll just wash my hands," Al says and turns. I kick her in the bum and she gets mad and turns round and says, "That's not fair. That's not part of the game."

"It is," I say. "Mummy did that to Daddy."

"She did not," Al says.

"Who says it has to be exactly the same?" I tickle her and she almost falls out of the tree. She climbs down and I run after her and we roll through the grass until we're out of breath.

Then we climb back up the tree and we smoke ivy and we both choke because it's damp from the rain but it's fun.

I hear a noise and tell Al to be quiet. The steps are coming closer and closer. Suddenly, I see someone wearing a blue shirt that looks just like my father's and a brown felt hat. But his walk is completely different. He does not swing his head from side to side like the pendulum of a clock. With each step it looks like he's sinking into the ground. As he passes directly beneath us, I see that his hat is torn. I can see part of his bald head. He walks on but then circles back. Al makes a noise and he looks straight up at us. He spits onto the grass. One of his eyes is made of glass. It's blue and bulges out. I recognize him as the tramp we saw the first day.

As soon as he leaves, Al and I race back to the house. We don't tell anyone about the man. Mum would get upset if we told her. She probably wouldn't believe us. She'd think we had imagined the whole thing. Juliet would tell us off and say it was our fault for going so far away. Same for Ethel. And Granny would just worry. "Cross your heart and hope to die," I say to Al.

Mummy bought us new dresses. Mine is black velvet while Al's is red. The collars and the cuffs are trimmed with satin. Mummy let me use her lipstick and Granny lent me a pair of stockings. I feel very grown up.

We've never been inside the doctor's house. It's very bare except for his bookcases which cover almost every wall. It's filled with things he's made. Like a wood lamp with a shade. He even makes boats he puts into glass bottles. He has a whole wall of boats in bottles. He shows us photographs of his boys. They don't look like him. They have dark brown hair and brown eyes and they're very handsome. He says to make ourselves comfortable in the living room, but his couch is very hard. It feels more like a bench.

Mummy tries to entertain us by telling us stories about the doctor. She says that the doctor is just like her because he loves children. In the night when his children were babies and cried, he got up. He used to drive his oldest son round and round for hours to get him to fall asleep, then he would tiptoe up the stairs and just as he was about to put him down in the crib his son would wake up.

We can hear all sorts of pans clattering in the kitchen.

"Are you all right in there?" Mummy asks.

"Fine," he answers.

"Are you sure you don't need help?" Mummy says.

"No," he says. "Dinner's ready."

We eat in the kitchen. The doctor places an enormous dish of pommes frites on the square wood table, and two chickens that are so cooked they fall apart on the dish. Mummy gets to serve herself first, then Al does. She piles more and more pommes frites onto her plate even though I kick her under the table. There are hardly any left for the doctor or me. When Mummy notices, she makes Al put some back. "I'm terribly sorry," she says to the doctor.

Then Al says that the doctor has a nose like an elephant. The doctor laughs but Mummy goes bright red. "Really, Al. The things you say."

The doctor doesn't close his mouth when he chews his food. I saw some of his pommes frites mashed up. He slurps his wine.

"We saw a tramp today," Al says.

"You promised," I lipsing to her. "No we didn't," I say.

"Yes, we did," she says.

"What did he look like?" The doctor asks.

"He had a glass eye," Al says.

"I think I know who you mean. For some reason everyone calls him Gauguin. Who knows why?" the doctor says. "He's been walking around the neighborhood for years."

Mum asks the doctor whether he has ever played Beethoven's Hammerklavier and he says he hasn't for many years. "I'm thinking of trying to play it," she says. "I remember playing it as a young girl in boarding school." They discuss the different movements and how they should be played. "Not too fast," the doctor adds.

"Don't worry," Mummy says. " My technique is so rusty." I didn't know that the doctor knew music as well as poetry. We've never heard him play. Al and I lipsing boring, boring, until Mum says we can be excused from the table.

While Mummy is in the kitchen helping the doctor clean up, Al and I open drawers and flip through books. We find a bound copy of *Anna Karenina* by the doctor's bedside table. Inside I read the inscription, "To my only love, Claire." At first I think it must be another Claire, but then I realize it's got to be Mummy.

Al and I are having a midnight feast in the kitchen. We're sitting at the round white table having our favorite: baguette and butter and chocolate Nesquick. It's completely dark except for the flashlight I'm holding, directed towards my face so that Al can see what I'm saying. Then I hear footsteps. They're very heavy. They sound like Juliet's but they're different. I place my finger over my lips, then turn off the flashlight. I stay as still as I can.

I can just make out Juliet's outline in the doorway. She takes a few steps and bumps into my chair but doesn't notice me. She continues over to the fridge. She opens the door. She's wearing flip-flops I've never seen before. She reaches inside the fridge.

Thirteen

Mummy is sitting in the doctor's lap in the piano room. She is stroking the top of his head. "Doudou," she says.

"Doudou," he says. I watch them kiss.

"I'm enjoying *Ivanov* so much," Mummy says. "It seems as if he is writing about today."

"*Uncle Vanya* is a much better play," the doctor says. "Checkhov is my favorite. I like him better than Tolstoy even."

"Surely not more than *Anna Karenina*," Mummy says.

"Even *Anna Karenina*," he says.

I read *Anna Karenina* to impress Mum and Dad. I found it very boring, but it was better than *Middlemarch*. Dad forced me to read *Middlemarch* last summer because he says I must stop reading romance novels.

Max is resting his head on the doctor's feet.

As I run out of the house, Juliet sticks her head out of her window. Al's up in her tree, but she doesn't see me. I just sit and poke a scab on my knee with a stick. I watch it bleed. Some pus comes out.

"Let's play," Al says, noticing me.

"I don't feel like it," I say.

"Let's play jumping into the river from the highest branch," she says.

"No," I say. "I don't feel like it."

I wait until she's not looking my way, then I pull out an atlas from a hole in the tree. The page is stained with blackberry juice, water, and grass. It doesn't matter because I know it by heart. Even the smallest river. They taught us to learn maps at school.

Mummy and the doctor are running along the bank of silver willows. I hurry to hide my book and the teacups. I throw sticks at Al and she hides the pots and pans under the blankets. Soon Mummy and the doctor stand beneath our trees. I peer down at them. Mummy laughs, holding her sides. She doesn't seem to see us.

"I beat you," she says.

"It's not entirely fair," the doctor says. "You had a—"

"I was just teasing," she says. She turns and kisses the doctor on the lips. Al leans further out of the tree. She almost falls out and they look up.

"Ooh, Al, you gave me a fright," Mummy says.

"I think we all deserve a treat," the doctor says. "Let's go into Malsherbes."

"What a lovely idea," Mummy says.

"I don't feel like it," I say.

"Come on, Gabriel," Mummy says. "We'll buy you some of those marzipan animals that you love so much."

"They're for babies," I say.

"Come on, sweetheart," Mummy says, holding out her hand. But I won't come. I stare at the water instead, at the leaves churning round and round.

I watch Al walk between them along the bank of silver willows. She holds their hands. Once she turns back and I think I can hear her hearing aid squeak but it's my tree. My tree is almost hollow inside and the ivy is so thick it hardly lets in any light.

The wind blows and the branches bend. Some of the trees are bent one way, while others are bent another. I pull out my atlas again and tear out the page. I let it drop onto the water. It floats a few feet, then it's sucked under just like the leaves.

Granny and Aunt Ethel are sitting in the blue foldout chairs beneath the willow tree outside Ethel's room. They do not see me run into the house. I wander from room to room. I walk into Granny's and open one drawer. I touch her pale pink petticoats. They're made of silk. I open her jewelry box and pull out her necklaces. She's let me play with her jewelry ever since I was a baby. Then I see her handbag sitting on the pink armchair. The clasp makes a loud clicking noise each time I open or close it. Ethel's voice drifts through the open door. "It's your life," she says. The curtains lift in the breeze and I catch a glimpse of Granny and Ethel's skirts and legs. I press myself against the wall. They do not turn and continue to knit.

"Can you believe it?" Ethel asks. "We've been here almost a month and a half."

"Really?" Granny says. "It seems more like a few days and at the same time like a year."

"Exactly a month and nine days," Ethel says.

Inside Granny's handbag, I find a silver cigarette lighter, a handkerchief, and a large pink wallet. I open her wallet and thumb through the bills. She's very rich. She has hundreds and hundreds of francs. The money smells of Granny. I take a one-hundred bill, then another and another. I slip the money into my pocket, replace her wallet, and close the bag.

Granny calls me after her nap. She asks me to help her make her bed; then we sit on the water lily couch. She's just wearing her petticoat. I keep putting my hand in my shorts and feeling the money.

"It's so exciting that you have your whole life ahead of you," she says. "I wonder what you will be."

"I don't know. I'd like to be a ballet dancer, but I think I'm going to be too big."

"I think there are some tall ballet dancers."

"But I might be very very tall like Daddy."

"That would be nice," Granny says. "I've always thought it would be nice to be tall. Anyway, you have plenty of time to decide."

I help Granny change into her mauve crocheted dress with long sleeves. She asks me to look through her jewelry box, a green satin box she bought in China. I choose a purple cross on a gold chain.

"What about this one?" I ask. "I've never seen you wear it."

She lifts the chain into the light so that the sun turns the stones purple.

"It's just garnets. My very first boyfriend gave this to me," Granny says. "I'd like you to have it, Gabriel."

She places the necklace in my palm. It's very light. I wonder if it was her first fiancé who gave it to her, the one Mum told us never to ask Granny about. Granny got married, but her parents had her marriage annulled. I wish I hadn't taken the money.

"It's quite warm today," Granny says, sitting down, waving her mauve hat in front of her face like a fan. I ask her if I can do it for her and she says, yes.

"What happened to the flowers on your hat?" I ask.

"I didn't notice," Granny says.

"They're all gone."

"What a shame," Granny says. "Well, it doesn't really matter. I only wear it to protect my face from the sun."

Gradually, the walls turn pink. The gold door knob gleams. From time to time, Granny closes her eyes, but when I ask her if she's sleeping she says she's just resting.

* * *

I'm lying on my bed, staring up at the ceiling when I hear grownups whispering outside my door.

"We must," Juliet says.

"I think it would be—" Granny says.

"Then she will think it's perfectly all right," Ethel says. "I can't believe you weren't going to say anything."

The door opens. Juliet, Ethel, Mummy, and Granny crowd through the doorway. Juliet holds my shorts.

"Young lady," Juliet advances towards my bed. I move back, thinking she's going to hit me, but she doesn't probably because the other grownups are here.

I look down at the crocheted blanket. It's got red and black and yellow and blue mixed in.

"Darling," Mummy says. "I don't understand why you would do such a thing."

"Stealing is a sin," Ethel says.

I thread my fingers through the holes in the crocheted squares. I can't bear to look at Granny.

"And to Granny of all people," Mummy says.

Granny holds my hand. She squeezes it tight. I can feel her rings dig into my hand.

"Never mind," Granny says.

"Never mind?" Ethel says. "What do you mean never mind?"

"She must be punished," Juliet says.

"Yes," Ethel says.

"I don't know," Mummy says.

"Perhaps it was a—" Granny says.

"Absolutely," Juliet says.

"Okay," I say, pulling the sheet with the crocheted blanket over my head.

120

Fourteen

The restaurant is dark and filled with smoke. It's called Le Lievre et le Faisan, The Hare and the Pheasant. On the walls hang paintings of hunting scenes. It even has glass ashtrays with a hare and a pheasant and a gun drawn in red. Al and I are the only children. We're wearing our red dresses with the green stems down the front and white petals for collars. This is the last time I'll be able to wear this dress. Juliet had to leave the top button undone. Mummy didn't understand why we wanted to wear them. She wanted us to wear the new ones.

Mummy keeps playing with her gold locket, squeezing it open and shut, making a clicking noise. "I'm so lucky to have you two girls," she says.

Al and I are sitting on the same red banquette. We're holding hands beneath the white tablecloth. We're twins again. I'm wearing one of her hearing aids. When Juliet told Al to put the other ear mold into her ear, Al said she couldn't because she has a huge pimple so Juliet couldn't say anything.

I like wearing a hearing aid. At first it felt funny in my ear, but now it feels nice. Al calls her hearing aid her ears. I have three ears now. Aunt Ethel said I was going to stretch it like a shoe.

The waiter asks if we have decided what we want and Mummy asks for one more minute.

"Would you like to order your food in reverse?" She asks us. She means starting with dessert and then having our entree and then the appetizer. She and her sister used to do that when they were little.

"No thank you," I say.

"Very well," she says. "Maybe we had better not, anyway. This place is so fancy."

Al and I order the exact same thing: salad to start with little nuts, then steak au poivre with French fries and Bearnaise sauce.

As soon as the waiter turns away from our table, Mummy lets go of her gold locket and says very fast, "Girls, what do you think of Xavier?"

I stare at the white cloth.

"He's okay," I say.

Al kicks the table leg and the water in the glasses almost spills. For a second, I thought it was me.

"What about Daddy?" Al asks.

"Is Daddy still in Brussels with his lady?" I say.

Mummy looks down at her plate and twists it round a bit. "Actually, he lives in Paris with Françoise."

"You mean he never lived in Brussels?" I ask.

"No."

"Where in Paris?" I ask

"On Rue du Dragon," Mummy says.

I imagine a narrow street with a big red dragon sticking out of one building.

"Xavier and I are going to go away for a few days," Mummy says.

"When?" I ask.

"Tomorrow, just for the week-end."

We eat our steak frites in silence. Everyone else is talking and laughing very loudly. The smoke is so thick I can hardly see the people at the table opposite us. I guess I stared too much at them because the man suddenly waved at me.

We have coffee with vanilla ice cream. Mummy didn't want to let us have coffee, but then she did.

The waiter brings the check on a silver plate in a black book with the same red sign on its jacket as the ashtrays. Mummy looks inside her navy blue handbag with the gold H; then she empties it onto the white tablecloth. There's an old metro ticket, a dirty Kleenex, a blue necklace, a toothpick, and a compact case. She searches through every pocket.

"Oh dear," she says. "What are we going to do? I don't have any money. Not even a carte de credit or check. I suppose I could call Xavier but that would be—"

"What about Granny?" I ask.

"She's probably in bed by now," Mummy says. "She doesn't have a car."

"Luis—"

"That would be even worse. Can you imagine—"

"Maybe if you talk to the manager. Remember the time when we were in Italy and you forgot your handbag at the hotel—" I say.

"Do you want me to ask him?" Al asks.

"No, no, darling, that's very sweet," Mummy answers. "I suppose I could try." She looks over at the owner who stands on the other side of the room. He's got very broad shoulders and his hair is greased. He sees Mummy staring at him and marches over. "Madame, is there a problem with the addition?"

"Oh no, no," Mummy says, staring into her handbag. "You see, I seem to have forgotten my wallet. I don't have any money or carte de credit or even personal checks."

For a moment, he doesn't say anything, but then he whispers, one eyebrow rising. "I suppose we'll have to put you to work cleaning the dishes." He laughs, then our mother laughs and I make a pretend laugh. "You two will have to wash the dishes." He laughs again.

He places his hand on Mummy's arm.

"Don't worry," he says. "I have complete confidence. Your husband is a regular. We haven't seen him lately. Send him my best regards."

"Yes, yes, yes," Mummy says, getting up hurriedly from the table. She rushes out of the restaurant with her handbag wide open. The man follows us. "Bonsoir," he says, holding the door.

"That was awful. Just awful," Mummy says.

It reminds me of the time the police stopped her in Paris and asked for her driving license. All she could find in the glove compartment was a tape that had come unwound. She kept pulling the tape, the gray ribbon growing longer and longer until it was completely unwound. The policeman didn't give her a ticket in the end.

"I suppose your father must have gone to that restaurant with Françoise," she says.

Al and I don't say anything. All I can hear is the wind rushing through the windows. The fields are lit by the moon. Now and then I reach out and write something across Al's palm. We've decided to call each other by the same name. We use the name that Mum and Dad used to call each other when they were teasing. Prue and Prue.

The house is dark except for a light in the living room. Granny is asleep in the blue and white striped chair. She's snoring very loudly. Al says she can hear it. Mummy can't decide whether or not to wake her. I say we should because otherwise she'll get a crick in her neck. "Granny," I say, placing my hand on her arm as I always do. She opens her arms and Al and I rush into them. She smells of her cream and of apricots. She says the two of us can sleep in her bed. "After all," she says, "tonight is special."

She lets us stay up very late. She makes us laugh by telling us stories about how when she was a young girl she turned down a boy who asked her to marry him because his ears were too big, then she tells us about the time she was on the QEII and this lady said, "Excuse me Ma'am," pointing to her chest and she looked down and realized that her boob had slipped out of her dress. The funniest story is the one about the bee that landed on this waiter's head. Granny waved her hand in the air to brush it off and she ended up brushing off his toupee. Al and I didn't know what a toupee was.

Fifteen

Even when Mummy stands in the doorway, half in the sun and half in the shade, I think she'll change her mind and decide not to go with the doctor after all. She's wearing her pale peach outfit with the pearl buttons down the front. She reaches up with one hand and touches the two dark red roses pinned to the brim of her hat.

"I hope I haven't forgotten anything," Mummy says, staring over her shoulder into the cool shadowy house. "I'm always forgetting something. Goodbye, Juliet." She stretches out her right hand but then changes her mind and kisses Juliet lightly on both cheeks.

"Don't worry," Juliet says, as she straightens her collar. She has done her dress up wrong so that there is no buttonhole for the top button.

"You're only going for a few days," Granny says. She places her hand on my shoulder.

"Even if you have forgotten something, it won't be the end of the world," Ethel says.

Mummy bends over and kisses me. Her cheek is soft like a plum. "You be good and remember that your Mummy loves you." I hold onto her tight but then I let go. She gets into the car and rolls down the window. "I'll call every day," she shouts over the sound of the car. We run alongside and then behind the car. We stop only at the top of the hill. We watch the car cut through gold fields, its back window glinting. It disappears into a dip and reappears a little later before disappearing once more. Al and I walk slowly down the hill, kicking a stone. First I kick the stone, then Al kicks it. We kick it all the way to the gravel courtyard.

We wander through the garden along the bank of silver willows, past our treehouse. We run through the field and find a Shetland Pony. He's wild and won't let us ride him. He tries to kick us if we come close. Then he disappears.

Al says we should play in our treehouses, but I tell her that

125

treehouses are for babies. Dolls too. "What about pretend?" she asks.

"Pretend too," I say.

I persuade her that we must get rid of our toys: the big and the small dolls, her toy monkey with the head that falls off and no longer squeaks, and my yellow rabbit that has sponge coming out of his nose. Daddy bought the rabbit for Mummy when I was still in Mum's stomach. He bought it yellow because he didn't know if I was going to be a boy or a girl. I tell Al that we can give them a proper burial. We wrap them in Al's white blanket with the blue flowers and then we place them in a cardboard box and we tie string around it. We dig a hole under a tree in the remains of the burnt house. Then we place the box in the hole. We make a cross out of two sticks. We don't know any prayers because we haven't been to church for years. We kneel in the earth and then we cross ourselves the way Catholics do. I say, "au nom du père, du saint esprit" and then I can't remember the rest.

***

"Girls," Granny calls from across the bank. "Why don't you come for a swim?" We walk across the lawn with our legs tied together by a string.

We watch Ethel get into the pool. First, she tests the water with the toes of one foot. Then she bends over and wets her hand which she runs over her chest and arms. She slowly eases herself into the water, and says "Ooh" as she lets herself drop. She swims with her neck straining upwards because she doesn't want to get her hair wet even though she's wearing a bright pink cap with plastic leaves. Granny is already swimming. She doesn't wear a cap. Max follows her up and down the pool, and Juliet lies in the sun in her new bikini.

Al and I jump in without untying the string from our legs. We don't even take off our T-shirt and shorts. "Girls," Juliet says. "What on earth are you doing?"

"We wanted to see what it would be like to swim with our clothes on, " I say.

It's hard swimming with one of your legs attached to someone else's leg. We splutter and pretend to drown. Then we stay in the shallow part.

"Juliet, why don't you come for a swim?" Granny asks.

"Yes," Ethel says. "It's such a hot day."

"Juliet doesn't know how to swim," I say.

"Of course I do," she mutters.

"If you don't know how, we could teach you," Granny says.

"It's not that hard, Juliet," Al says. "You just kick your arms and legs."

"I have no use for swimming," she says.

"But what if you were on a boat and it got shipwrecked?" I ask.

"At least come for a dip in the shallow end," Granny says.

Juliet's face is bright red. I thought she was crying but she said it was sweat dripping into her eyes.

She gets up slowly and walks on tiptoes across the lawn. She dips her foot in the pool. She wets her hand and arms just like Ethel, but then she just stands there.

"Come on, Juliet," I say.

"Come on," Al says.

She stares at her shadow in the water, then walks round the side to the ladder. She goes down one step, then another. We all gather around her. I have to keep pushing Max out of the way.

"That dog," Juliet says.

"Yes," Ethel says. "They never should have allowed him in the pool in the first place."

"Let me see," Granny says. "How should we start?"

"Juliet must hold onto the side and kick," I say.

"Excellent idea," Granny says.

Juliet kicks, but so slowly she would drown if she weren't holding onto the edge.

"Harder," I say.

"Harder," Al says.

She kicks a bit faster, but then she says she's tired. She just wants to relax.

"The most relaxing is to float on your back," I say.

"We'll hold you," Al says.

At first Juliet says she doesn't want to. I wonder if it reminds her of her brothers forcing her to fall on her back. Then Granny and Ethel say they will help us.

They hold her shoulders and her head, while we hold her legs.

"Are you ready?" we ask.

"Not just yet," she answers. She doesn't want to put her head back completely into the water.

"One. Two. Three." We let go and she floats. She floats and floats. She looks like a man with her hair all wet and her beaked nose sticking up in the air.

Al and I untie our string and I tell Granny to play a game of floating. Who can stay the longest floating? Ethel's the only one who won't do it because of her hair. We try to turn Max onto his back but he barks and scratches us with his long nails. He climbs out of the pool using the ladder, then lies in the sun licking himself.

We lie on our backs and float, looking up at the sky. The clouds look like my mother and father. I recognize in one cloud the shape of my father's nose and his hat, in the edge of another, my mother's profile. I float for a long time, but when I stand up Juliet is still floating.

***

Al and I found all these seeds in the garage for growing flowers. They come in small white packets with the pictures of flowers. We're going to plant them in the remains of the burnt house, right where we buried our dolls, my yellow rabbit and Al's monkey and her white blanket. We're going to put them there even though Granny told us they need to be in the sun. They're just going to have to grow in the shade. Cemeteries always have flowers. We have a shovel but mostly we use our hands. I like the earth that's below the surface because it's cool. I don't like worms. Al's in charge of pulling them out and dropping them into a bucket, then emptying the bucket into the river. We spend a long time planting the seeds. We don't notice Juliet and Luis standing beneath the willow tree until we get up to go back to the house. All we can see are their ankles and their feet. Luis is wearing his black shoes. His feet are on either side of Juliet's bare feet. We watch Juliet rub the back of her calf with one foot. I think they're kissing.

***

"Come," Granny says, when I go into her room after her nap. She's already dressed and sitting in her pink armchair. She shoves her knitting into her green bag and pulls on her straw hat. She grabs my hand and we rush out the door. She stops. The swimming pool is pink, and the sun about to disappear. You can see just a sliver of red. We climb the hill slowly and Granny leans quite heavily on my shoulder, but I don't mind. We wander through the arcade of trees, up the stone steps covered with moss, past mushrooms which have grown at the foot of trees. I think I hear the sound of wings fluttering, but when I turn there's only the movement of a branch swinging back into place.

In the vegetable garden the earth looks orange and the grass blue. A patch of wild strawberries has grown. The tomatoes look as if they're about to burst. Some have dropped and cracked open. Others are ready to fall. I glance over my shoulder to catch the sun before it dips, but it's already disappeared. In the distance, through branches, the river flickers gold.

Usually, Granny kicks off her shoes, but tonight she's having trouble reaching her toes. I take off first one purple shoe then the other. The purple dye has bled onto her stockinged feet. I help her slide up her skirt and unhook her stockings. As I sit down beside her, she says, "Everything is such an effort when you get old." She slips one hand down the front of her dress and pulls out a pack of cigarettes. She slides one out carefully and reaches into her pocket to take out her silver lighter. She lights her cigarette and inhales deeply.

She takes my hand and holds it in her other hand. Granny says she knew when she first saw me that we would get along. She says she can tell with people right away. Someone can walk into the same room as her and she can tell whether she will like them or not, before they've even spoken. Granny lets me try on her rings. One is green, one is yellow, and one is pale blue.

"I like the blue one best," I say.

"Do you? I think I do too. It's the one I've had the longest time."

"Did you buy it or did grandfather?"

"It happened so long ago," Granny says. She reaches out and eats a small tomato whole. "Once upon a time there was a very young and foolish girl who fell madly in love with a young man. She disregarded her sisters' warnings and ran away."

"You ran away?"

"Yes," she says. "But then I changed my mind."

"Why did you change your mind?"

"I realized I was too young to assume such a responsibility," she says.

I think I understand what Granny means and I nod because I love it when she talks to me like a grownup. She talks to me as if I were exactly her own age.

I try to picture what her first boyfriend looked like, but a photograph of my grandfather comes to mind. He was much older than Granny. He was bald and plump.

"Would you like me to pick you some strawberries?" I ask Granny.

"Oh, yes," Granny says. "That would be lovely."

Wild strawberries are Granny's favorite fruit apart from figs. I walk over to the other side of the garden. I can still see Granny from where I am. She's moved so that now she's in the shade of a tree.

With one hand I hold the hem of my dress, with the other I pick and drop strawberries into my skirt. It's going to take a long time to pick enough strawberries for the two of us. I think of the trip Granny promised me. I see the QEII, a giant white ship cutting through blue waves, and Granny and me sitting on deck wrapped in blankets and sipping consomme. We'll go around the world. Sometimes I glance over my shoulder and Granny waves to me and her rings catch the sun. Sometimes she does not see me look at her and I watch her pop another tomato into her mouth. I sing an Afrikaans song that Granny taught me. "Liefste Tannie ons bring rosies. Rosies blink met more dou."

At last my skirt is full and I turn back. I walk slowly, holding my skirt with both hands, my eyes fixed on the strawberries. I don't want any to spill. When I look up, the sky is mauve and the grass almost turquoise. Granny is sleeping with her back leaning against a tree. Her dress has slid up and I can see her knees which look very white. Her hands rest in her lap. The wind blows and one of her stockings drifts away a few feet. In the shadow of the tree her face looks very pale. She never goes in the sun because she says it's bad for your skin. Her hat lies face down on the grass. I place one hand on her arm as I always do and whisper into her ear, "Granny." She does not move. I say it again much louder. I lean closer. I can smell her powder and her cream. I shake her.

"Granny. Granny. Granny. Granny," I scream.

Strawberries lie all around her, even on her, in her lap and sprinkled in her hair. I sit down beside her and rest my head on her shoulder. I can hear her heart fluttering. It flutters louder and louder, but there's no pulse in her neck and I realize that it's my own heart I'm hearing.

Shadows drift across the grass. The sky darkens and the grass becomes wet and soon my dress is damp. The birds are quiet, the garden hushed and still. The dew on Granny's arm feels cold. If I don't move, not even to brush away the grass tickling my leg, everything will be all right. Then Max comes sniffing around us. He puts his wet nose between Granny and me, and I push him away, but he keeps circling us. He flops down beside us and begins to howl. I tell him to stop being a stupid dog, shut his mouth. Then I get up because I see something glimmering in the grass. It's Granny's silver lighter. When I look over at Granny, she looks like another lady.

I run down the hill, but then I stop and walk back up. Granny is very heavy and I only attach the stockings to the front hooks. I slip on her shoes. I pull down the skirt of her dress over her knees. I'm about to place her hat on her head when the wind blows, making it somersault through the air. I run after it, catching it just before it touches the ground. Three streaks of pink run from Granny's jaw to her chest, as if she had drawn her hand down her neck. I dig a hole beneath the laburnum tree and hide the last two cigarettes inside.

***

All I can see, lying flat on the bottom of my canoe, is the sky and the branches overhanging the river. I listen to the sound of water lapping against the sides of my boat. I don't know how long I've been floating. I try not to think of Granny.

I sit up. Now I can see mansions that seem to be made out of pink and gray paper glued together. I float beneath trees that do not hang over the river but lean away, as if they don't like the river, or cannot bear to see their own reflections.

I'm hungry, but all I have is one old caranbar. I suck on it slowly. I'm now drifting down a narrow bend which finally ends in a pond filled with mud. There is nothing to do but climb out. I let the air out of my canoe and then I fold it up and place it under one arm.

I walk along the road singing a French song I learned in ski school. "Un kilomèters à pied ça use, ça use. Un kilomèters à pied ça use les souliers. Deux kilomèters à pied ça use ça use." I walk along a very big highway. I don't know where I'm going. Cars keep passing me. A man in a gray bakery van stops and asks me if I need a lift, but I say "non, merci" and he drives on. The smell of the baguettes stays in the air. I try to smell it for as long as I can.

I walk and walk until my legs are sore.

A police van pulls up beside me.

"Où tu vas comme ça?" the policeman who sits behind the wheel asks.

"Je vais voir ma grandmère," I say.

"Et où elle habites, ta grandmère?" he asks.

"Pres d'Estouy," I say.

"Mais c'est trèsloin. Allez, on va t'emmener," he says.

I climb into the car.

I stare at their backs. The policeman who sits behind the wheel keeps twisting his neck to see me. The other policeman is talking, but I can't hear what he says because he's got the radio on and it's all static. He keeps waving his hands in the air.

"Why were you running away?" The policeman who keeps looking back at me asks.

"I wasn't," I say. I stare through the window at the poplars. The wind blows through them turning them silver. "I just wanted to go down the river in my canoe."

"Next time I would advise you not to go so far," the other policeman says. His nose is as red as Aunt Ethel's cheeks.

"Your parents must be very worried about you," he says.

"My mother's dead," I say.

"I'm sorry," he says. "Your father will be waiting for you, then?"

"He's dead too," I say. "They both died of scarlet fever. I'm an orphan."

"Do you have any brothers or sisters?"

"They died too, and even my governess," I say. "I live with my grandmother."

***

We are all seated in the living room: Aunt Ethel and Mummy and the doctor and the two policemen. Through the open door, I can see Juliet playing hide and seek with Al. Al is hidden behind a bush and Juliet is pretending not to be able to see her. I watch Juliet come around the bush where Al is hiding. She says very loudly, her words drifting over to us, "I think I'll have to give up. You just hide too well for me."

The doctor is holding Mummy's hand. Her face is sad. The last of the sunlight catches the top of her head. Everything in the room gleams, the gold bearings of the curtains, the flower bowl, even aunt Ethel's needles.

"I see you," Juliet shouts, catching Al in her arms, as Al jumps out from behind the bush. "I've found you."

The policemen stand and shake hands, then the doctor sees them out.

"It's my turn now," Juliet says. "No peeking. Keep your eyes closed."

I slip out the living room, walk slowly up the stairs to my room. It's too early to sleep. I run my hand over the wallpaper and pop as many bumps as I can. Soon there aren't any left within my reach.

I wait and wait to feel Granny tickle the bottom of my foot, but she never comes. Later, Al climbs up into my bunk bed. She writes across my palm that she knows where Juliet hid the canoe. Next time we'll escape together. But I'm thinking about Granny, wondering if she called me while I was picking the strawberries.

133

Sixteen

The pink and yellow flowers of the curtains seem to be slowly circling, swirling, drifting off into the air. I have the feeling, even though I'm lying as still as I can on my back, that I'm floating. Everything is floating except for my head which aches. The slightest movement makes it throb. At times, I manage to escape. I float outside of my body and look down from one corner. Yes, that's me with the long arms and legs and the brown hair and green eyes.

When I close my eyes, I feel as if I'm drowning, sinking deeper and deeper into the water. It's a pleasant feeling, except that for a moment I wonder if I'm dying. I know that I'm ill. From time to time, my body trembles and my teeth chatter and I'm terribly cold and wish someone would pile blankets over me. Then the next moment, I'm so hot, my face is covered with perspiration and the sheet sticks to my back and I would give anything for a cool cloth.

I don't see Juliet enter the room. Suddenly I feel her wide rough hand upon my forehead. She rolls me over, first one way, then the other. I'm conscious of cool clean sheets. "You have a good sleep," she says.

Later I'm aware of her sitting by the window. Gradually, I can make out the outline of her back and head, the ladder of the chair. She's darning.

She leans out the window and smokes.

Still later I hear voices. A man's. I think it's my father standing in the doorway, but then I hear the doctor say, "There's nothing to worry about. Children often have high fevers." I let myself drop again. It feels a bit like falling without landing. I watch shadows grow, then shrink.

Sometimes I think it's been four or five hours since Juliet's come in but when I ask her, she says it's only been half an hour. At other times, I think she's just been out of the room for a minute and it's been several hours. Sometimes I can feel that someone is standing in the doorway, but it's too much trouble to open my eyes.

Several times I'm sure I can sense my father's presence. I recognize each hand: mother's which is soft and smells of her cream, Al's which is always sticky with jam or honey or something she has eaten, Juliet's which is wide and heavy. Once I even felt Ethel's small dry hand. It smells of peppermint. I keep waiting to feel Granny's hand, so different from all the others, heavy because of her rings, but light. I thought I felt her tickle the bottom of my foot, but it was Max. He likes to sleep at the bottom of my bed. Juliet shoos him off and he lies on the blue carpet, but as soon as her footsteps have faded he jumps back up.

Later, much later, the doctor reappears. This time he's alone. He sits down on the edge of my bed. He has to bend his head because of the top bunk bed. "How are you feeling?" he says.

"All right."

"I remember when my grandmother died," he says. "I was so upset because we were supposed to go on a picnic the very next day. I had looked forward to it for weeks and weeks."

I stare at his narrow face. Even his nose and his eyes are narrow.

"What was her name?" I ask.

"Anne," he says.

"Granny's name was Whilelmina."

"I was very angry with her for a long time," he goes on. "I thought that somehow she could have chosen not to die."

"But she couldn't," I say.

"No," he says. "She couldn't."

I close my eyes and pretend that I'm floating down the river in my canoe. I don't hear the doctor tiptoe out.

In the night I awaken to singing. It's Juliet. Her voice is hoarse as if she has been singing for a long time. Then it sounds like she's talking to someone. She's having an argument. "I'm not going to go through this again. Do you understand?" She stomps around. I'm sure that the floorboards over Granny's room are shaking. I picture her room with the shutters open and the moonlight across the red rug and the waterlily couch, Tiger stretched across Granny's empty pillow.

Seventeen

I can't tell if it's morning or evening. Juliet is still sitting in the same chair, but she's reading her book. Each time she turns a page it sounds very loud, as if I were wearing Al's hearing aid. "Well, I'll be—I never would have guessed," she says, throwing her mystery down. It lands with a small thud which wakes Max, who is lying on the blue carpet. A mystery is no good if Juliet can't figure out who did it.

"Juliet," I say, sitting up.

"Are you feeling better?" she asks, turning round her chair.

"Juliet, did Daddy come while I was sick?"

"No, but I think he called quite a few times."

Juliet does a few steps in front of the window as if she were rehearsing a dance, then sits down again.

"Juliet, did you really dance on points when you were a little girl?"

"Yes," she says, stretching her legs out and staring at her feet.

I try to imagine a tiny Juliet with dark curly hair and chubby legs wearing a bright red tutu and red toe shoes. She comes onto the stage carrying a tambourine with red ribbons. She pirouettes across the stage and everyone applauds except for her five brothers, who look bored, sitting in the front row.

"Tell me some more stories about your brothers," I say.

"You must be feeling better if you're asking me all these questions."

"Where are they? Do they all live in London?"

"John and Matthew and Luke live close to London, a little ways away," she says, bending over and picking up her mystery. There's a picture of an ax and a sword on the cover.

"And the other two?"

"They died. Arthur died when I was four. Jared, the day after the war ended. He was walking across the beach and there were mines. Blew him to pieces."

I try to imagine her brother blown into tiny pieces, but I can't.

Just the beach and the sand and the gray sea. I can imagine the sound of the sea because of the river. The river reminds me of Granny. I keep expecting her to step into my room. I wouldn't be surprised if she did. I picture her standing in the doorway wearing her mauve dress with the pleated skirt, fixing the cuffs of her sleeves.

"I'm going to bring you a nice bowl of consommé," Juliet says.

"I'm not hungry."

"You've got to eat something," she says, slowly getting up, still looking down though at the pale blue carpet with the white crosses, as if she could see her brother there.

"How long have I been sick?" I ask, expecting her to say three weeks, but she says that it has been only one day and one night.

As soon as she leaves the room, I throw back the sheet and slowly stand up. For a moment the floor seems to heave, but I steady myself on the bunk bed. I take a few steps across the blue carpet. I feel different, lighter and taller, as if I had grown while in bed.

***

Al and I are lying on a blanket with the branches of the willow tree over our heads so it looks like we've got green hair. Whenever Ethel or Mummy look my way, I let the branches drop and I'm hidden by a screen of green.

Every few minutes they get up to move their chairs and the white table into the shade. They've hardly said a word. Mum said something about being unable to find her place, and Ethel something about being afraid she's running out of beads.

That's because Al and I have her beads. We collected all the ones we could find and put them in a jar.

"She wouldn't want us to mope," Ethel says, looking up from her knitting.

"No," Mummy says. "She wouldn't."

Ethel picks up the silver teapot, but her hand shakes so hard tea splashes the white tablecloth, the one Granny and Ethel and Mummy embroidered the summer before. It has flowers and ladybirds and butterflies, all different colors. I helped sew the ladybird at its center.

"Oh dear," Ethel says, moving her chair back. "Look what I've done!"

"Oh dear," Mummy says, resting one hand on Ethel's arm. They both cry.

Mummy clasps Ethel's hand and says with a slight laugh, "But we're being ridiculous. It's just cloth. I'm sure that—"

"Such a steady hand," Ethel says. "Like a rock."

"What I can't get over is—"

"You know I think she was still smoking," Ethel says.

"I can't believe—" Mummy says.

"Yes, it's hard to believe. The doctors at home advised her not to come, but you know what she's like."

"But she seemed—" Mummy says.

"I have very high blood pressure, you know," Ethel says.

"Yes," Mummy says. She places the silver teapot, the teacups, the bowl of sugar, and the pitcher of milk on the lawn. She lifts the tablecloth off the table. "I'll just run in and soak it."

"Let me do it," Ethel says. "After all it's my fault."

"No, no," Mummy says.

I let the green curtain drop. Al's pretending to be dead. She lies still in the grass. I tickle her, but she doesn't move. Not even when I take a blade of grass and brush her neck. It makes me think of the time Dad climbed onto the top bunk and took the tip of his belt and let it brush Al's cheek and she kept brushing her cheek and Dad and I laughed.

"There," Mummy says. "It didn't take a minute. I'm sure it will come out."

"We haven't seen the doctor today," Ethel says.

"No," Mummy says.

"Such a nice man," Ethel says.

"I feel so guilty for not being here when—" Mummy says.

"Oh but there was nothing you could do." Ethel stands, bends over, and replaces the teapot, the tea cups and the pitcher of milk on the table.

"What about him?" Ethel asks lowering her voice. "Has he been calling again?"

"He says he's coming to the funeral," Mummy answers. "He was very fond of her despite their differences."

"To think that I don't even have to change the date of my ticket to S. A.," Ethel says.

138

"As if it were all planned, as if she knew," Mummy says. "Are you sure I can't persuade you to take the plane? We could travel together that way. It would be so much quicker."

"Oh no, my dear," Ethel says. "I cannot abide planes."

"Come over here, girls," Mummy calls. We push back the willow tree's branches and walk across the grass. I feel so tall and thin. I don't know what to do with my arms. They seem to be swinging the wrong way. Mummy hugs each of us with one arm.

"You're almost too big to sit on my lap."

"We are too big," I say.

"Well," Mummy says. "Not if you sit one at a time."

We take turns sitting on her lap.

"Gabriel has really shot up," Ethel says.

"No, I haven't," I say, jumping up from Mummy's lap before she finds me too heavy.

I walk over to the bridge which has lost its side. Now there's only a plank to walk across. I stare through the water at the wood. Already one piece has broken off and floated a short distance.

Later I see Ethel, teapot in hand, going from flower to flower. The silver teapot flashes in the sun. I follow her, and she keeps pouring tea onto the flowers. She says tea leaves are good for them. She pours from the teapot even when there is no tea left. If I were younger, I might think she was playing pretend.

Eighteen

Al's dressed up as a nurse. She's wearing a little white cap with a red edge, an apron, and a stethoscope.

"Lie down again," she says.

"Okay," I say. Her voice stays on one note because she had to take her hearing aids out to put in the stethoscope. She can't say stethoscope.

"Cough," she says, but I don't.

"Now turn your head." She peers into my right ear. "I'm going to test your reflexes." She produces a little hammer from her black bag and hits my knees.

"Moan," she says. "Groan."

"I told you. I don't feel like playing."

"Now, I'm going to put a suppository up your bum," she says.

"No, you're not," I say, jumping up. She runs after me. We run and run until I turn round and tell her to leave me alone or I'll never talk to her again.

I stop just outside Granny's room and peer through the window.

Ethel is walking back and forth between the chest of drawers and the couch. Granny's dresses are heaped over the back of one chair; her silk petticoats, bras, and corsets hang over the side of another. Her shoes have been placed side by side in a long line. Mummy's standing in the middle of the room. She says something but I can't hear what.

"You don't understand," Ethel says, as she places one of Granny's dresses flat into the suitcase. It's the blue-green one that looks like water.

"I do," Mummy says. "But we must bury her soon. It's been—"

Ethel continues to walk back and forth between the chest of drawers and the couch. Mummy continues to stand. She keeps touching Granny's pearls around her neck.

"She wore these to our wedding," Mummy says, touching the

140

pearls. "Do you remember?"

"She wore them almost every day of her life," Ethel answers.

Ethel turns her back to Mummy as she pulls out another drawer to the bureau and I climb onto the ledge outside Ethel's window. I pull myself up onto the green shutters. I stand on top of the green shutters, then swing up onto the ledge outside Juliet's window. She's had her door closed since this morning. It's her day off, but she didn't want to go for a drive with Luis.

Her room is the same as it was at the beginning of the summer. Books lie on the floor. Clothes are strewn across her bed and chair. Juliet's sitting on her bed. She's wearing her wig, but she's got it on back to front. She doesn't seem to notice as she combs it in place.

I climb down slowly. Al is waiting and I'm glad. I tell her about Ethel and Mummy arguing, Juliet wearing her wig back to front. We hold hands as we wander through the garden. Al says she doesn't need to look at me to understand what I'm going to say. She knows even before I've said it. That's why we're twins.

Every night Al and I get to sleep in Mummy's bed. She says we're a great comfort. I count the beams but I cannot fall asleep for a very long time. Sometimes, I see the morning light filter in. Mummy always falls asleep before me, but tonight she doesn't seem able to sleep either. She gets up from her bed and I think she's gone to pee, but then I hear a noise coming from below. I tiptoe downstairs through the living room. A silver shadow lights the portrait of the little girl above the mantelpiece. Her eyes seem to shift, as if she were following me with her gaze.

In the kitchen, I find Mummy sitting at the round kitchen table. There's no light except for a narrow beam from the refrigerator. "Hello, darling," she says.

"I can't sleep," I say.

"For some reason what I really feel like eating is a piece of biltong. Granny liked biltong."

"Did she?"

I'm not sure what biltong is. I seem to remember a long strand of dried beef.

"Me and Catherine used to have midnight feasts of baguette and rillettes," I say.

"I'm sorry she couldn't come this summer," Mummy says. "But I suppose with all that's been going on it's just as well." She cries and I put my arms around her. I feel like crying too, but no tears come. I concentrate on the smell of her hair like flowers. I wish I were smaller so I could sit on her lap. But I'm too big. I try to think of something funny to cheer Mummy up.

"Remember the time Juliet spanked my friend Catherine instead of me?"

"Did she really?" Mummy wipes her eyes.

"Yes," I say. "It was all dark so she couldn't see. She just reached for someone lying on the top bunk bed and she must have grabbed Catherine instead of me and she gave her a beating with her shoe."

"I'm surprised she didn't realize it wasn't you," Mummy says. She takes another sip of milk and now she has a big mustache.

"Juliet's different in the night," I say.

"Is she?" Mummy says. "How?"

"She sings and sometimes she cries."

"It must be hard being a nanny sometimes," she says.

"Mummy," I ask, "is Daddy coming to the funeral?"

"He might. He says he's coming. But I don't want you to be disappointed."

Nineteen

"Don't move," Juliet says. She is kneeling on the floor pinning my dress. It's so hot I feel faint. I think a lump is growing on each side of my chest. Juliet says that soon I'm going to have breasts. I'm praying they won't be as big as hers.

Through the window I can see the doctor, Mummy, Al, and Luis playing boules. At first Ethel was very disapproving when the doctor brought the boules over. "It doesn't seem right," she said. "The day of her funeral."

But the doctor went for a walk with Ethel and let her talk and talk even though he couldn't understand half of what she was saying because she talks so fast and when she got back and he suggested we play boules she said she didn't see any harm in watching. I think she was so happy that Mum let the doctor come over she didn't want to make too much of a fuss.

The boules are silver and reflect the sun. They make a special noise when they knock each other.

"My boule is definitely closer," the doctor says.

"No," Mummy says. "Mine is."

"I assure you——" and his face goes a bit red.

"We're not going to argue, are we?" Mummy says.

Daddy gets very mad when he looses at bridge. I don't like to play with him and Mummy because he gets so upset if he loses.

"Men are all the same," Juliet says. "Have you ever seen a woman get as upset over losing a game?"

"I do," I say. "I hate it when you or Al or anybody beats me."

"That's because you're still little," Juliet says.

"Not that little. Soon I'm going to be a teenager."

"Let me show you," the doctor says to Mummy. He swings his arm but his ball flies wide of the smaller ball.

"It doesn't seem to help you," Mummy laughs and looks back at the doctor. He wipes his brow with the back of his sleeve and smiles. I wonder if Mummy has agreed to marry him. His hair is as white as Granny's.

"Are you almost done?" I ask Juliet.

"Yes, yes, just stand still for another minute."

"Come and play boules," the doctor says.

"No thanks," I say. But then I feel badly because he looks disappointed.

"What about you, Juliet?" the doctor says.

"Oh no," she says. "I have to sew this hem."

***

Luis is driving slowly, but we do not mind. He does not make swerves in the road. He does not sing. He keeps his eyes fixed on the hearse where Granny lies. When the hearse dips, the purple curtains part, and the gold handle of the black coffin flashes in the sun.

Inside, the car is like a furnace. Even the breeze blowing through the open windows is hot and so dry that our lips are parched and our throats filled with dust. I don't even try to lift my leg or sit forward. Our clothes feel stiff and rough and the flowers I hold in my hand, Granny's favorite, Ghislaine de Feligonde, droop over my fingers, their heads resting on my lap.

Al let me wear both her hearing aids. Sometimes they hurt my ears because the sounds are so loud. I can't hear what anyone is saying because the background noise is too loud.

Ethel says that Granny is in heaven. Mummy says she does not know where she is, but that wherever she is she's lying peacefully. I don't believe either of them. I think she's sitting in another vegetable garden eating tomatoes and smoking cigarettes.

"If only she had listened to me," Ethel says. "Up at the crack of dawn to see roses and then every evening climbing that hill to the vegetable garden. Whatever for, I'd ask her."

Ethel's never been up to the vegetable garden. The only time she went was when Granny died.

"Do you know I think she was still smoking?" Ethel says.

"Yes," Mummy says. "You—"

"Sometimes I thought I could smell it on her clothes, but I never said anything because she got so angry when I did. But perhaps I should have. Perhaps—"

"Please," Mummy says.

Ethel opens her dark green bead bag, then snaps it shut. She sits absolutely still. Even when a gnat settles on her nose, she does not move. She bought the same black hat as Mummy except Ethel's hat has a long feather she had to bend in order to get into the car. Her hat looks like a dragonfly.

"How come Granny didn't live until ninety five like our great-grandfather?" Al asks. "He smoked a pack of cigarettes a day."

"Some people die sooner than others," Mummy answers.

"Will I die soon and you too?" Al asks.

"Not soon my sweet but one day we all will," Mummy says.

"Even Juliet?" Al says.

"Yes," Mummy says.

Juliet laughs, "She thinks I'm indestructible." Juliet keeps wiping her forehead. She's wearing a black dress, but it wasn't respectable enough so she had to wear a black cardigan over it. She keeps glancing up at the rearview mirror, but Luis stares straight ahead at the road. Al and I saw him cleaning the plastic that protects the photograph of his wife and children. He told us that he needed to have another photograph taken of them. They already look very different.

"What are you doing, Gabriel?" Ethel asks.

I look down and realize that I have been absentmindedly plucking the petals of Granny's roses so that now all that's left are the heads and drooping stems.

The air is so hot a thin haze covers the gold fields.

We stop in front of a small stone church. As we open the doors to the car, a string of swallows perched on a telephone wire fly up into the air, their breasts turning silver as they swerve towards the sun.

The church is cool and damp, dimly lit by candles. The stained glass windows throw blue and purple shadows onto the gray flagstones. Hundreds and hundreds of flowers fill the church. The scent is very strong and I think it's gone to Ethel's head because she rushes from bouquet to bouquet plucking out flowers, letting them drop onto the floor so that soon it's covered with yellow flowers. Holding my hand, Mummy rushes over to Ethel.

"What are you doing, Ethel?"

"She hated yellow," Ethel says.

"It doesn't matter anymore," Mummy says. We walk to the front row where Juliet and Al already stand. We are the only ones in the church except for the doctor and Luis who stand in the last row. Granny has lots of friends, but they couldn't come all the way from South Africa.

The service begins, but I can't understand what the minister is saying because he is so old and bent his chin touches his chest and his words seem to disappear inside of him. Ethel keeps leaning towards Mummy, asking, "What is he saying? What did he say?"

"Hush," Mummy says. "I can't understand myself."

Then I hear footsteps. It's my father. I knew he'd come. He lifts one hand and places one finger in front of his lips. The gold cufflink on his shirt glints as it passes through a ray of sun.

The minister keeps talking. Sometimes it sounds as if he is singing. I keep turning to see if my father is still there. The ray of sun has moved further and now he stands in the shade. His navy blue jacket and pants look black. He's wearing a pink shirt.

I stare at the yellow flowers on the gray flagstones. I never knew that Granny didn't like yellow. For some reason, the thought makes me sad.

"Come, come," the minister says, motioning slowly with one arm for us to move forward towards the coffin. Ethel grips me by the shoulder.

I peer over the side of the coffin. I don't recognize Granny. All her wrinkles are gone and her cheeks and eyes are puffed. Her mouth is drawn down. Her white face seems to float from within the purple ruffles framing it, but her brow, when I lean over and kiss it, feels like marble.

Outside the church, the light is blinding. Father bends over and kisses us on each cheek. "You're big girls now," he says, patting the tops of our heads. "I'm very sorry," he turns to shake Ethel's hand. "Yes," she says. His lips brush Mummy's cheek. Then he shakes hands with the doctor who looks down at the gravel.

"Juliet," Daddy says. "I hope you are well."

"Oh yes," Juliet says.

"I don't know what we would have done without Juliet," Mummy says. "She's been an absolute angel."

"An angel," Ethel repeats.

Juliet pretends not to care, but I can tell that she's stopping her-

146

self from smiling.

"Are they coming soon?" Al asks.

"Any minute now," Juliet says.

The doors open and four men come out of the church carrying the coffin. One of the men wears a gray tie with heads of people drawn in black. The coffin seems too big for Granny. I can't believe she's inside. What if she wakes up?

We follow the minister down a path made of tiny white pebbles. Al keeps picking up pebbles and slipping them into her pockets. By the time we get to the grave, her pockets are bulging. Some of the graves are so old there's only a sliver of the tombstone left, while the names and the dates of others have been washed off. Besides Granny's grave, there's a tombstone for a baby. The dates are April 1970 to May 1970.

The lawn is very green. It almost looks fake. Sprinklers water the lawns and we all have to rush down the path in order to avoid getting wet. The minister apologizes. The four young men carrying the coffin rush through the spray, but they still get wet. The forehead of one glistens. Another got his ear wet.

It looks like Granny's grave has been cut out, the edges are so neat and the rectangle so perfect. I wish they weren't burying her here, I know she would have preferred the vegetable garden. As the coffin is being lowered, our father cries very loudly and I look down at my shoes. They're black patent and reflect the grass. He cries and cries. Al holds my hand. I give her back her hearing aid.

The return walk along the white path seems longer even though we take exactly the same route. The sun is so strong it reflects off the path. I try to narrow my eyes.

I'm glad when we reach Luis's car. But he's sprayed it with more perfume.

"I don't feel so good," I say, leaning out the window.

"Why do you spray the car with so much deodorizer?" Ethel asks. "It's almost insulting."

"Insulting?" Luis asks.

"Like we all smell bad," Ethel says, holding her nose.

"No, no, no, Mrs. Ethel."

"I rather like it," Juliet says.

I hear the vroom noise my father's car always makes when it starts up. I turn and kneel on the seat and stare out the back window. He's following us. The road dips, then climbs and sometimes I think my father's gone, but then I catch a glimpse of him before his car disappears once again.

"Sit down properly," Ethel says. "I said, sit down properly." She pulls on the hem of my dress.

"Darling," Mummy says. "Will you please sit properly?"

My father drives past us.

"All right," I say.

I close my eyes and feel the car going up and dipping down. I try to imagine that I'm not in a car but in a ship. I imagine the cool blue water and the white froth, the sound of the boat hitting the waves.

"It seemed awfully short," Ethel says. "Too short. Didn't you think it seemed too short?"

"Yes, it did seem short," Mummy says.

"Did you think it was short, Juliet?" Ethel asks.

"I beg your pardon," Juliet says.

"Never mind," Ethel says.

I wish Ethel would stop talking. She's like a mosquito, circling round and round your head. Sometimes you think she's gone, but then you hear the droning in your ear and she stings you.

"Luis, didn't you think it was too short?" Ethel asks.

"Yes, Mrs. Ethel, too short."

"I was wondering if he would come," Ethel says.

"Yes," Mummy says.

"Luis, I think we have taken a wrong turn," Ethel says.

"Yes, Mrs. Ethel." He flicks his ear with one finger as if a fly had got in.

Brambles and wild rosebushes grow so far onto the road they scratch the sides of Luis's gold car. Luis keeps saying, "Madre de Dios," and wiping his brow with a white handkerchief. He continues going down the road, but the road becomes worse and worse, until it's no longer a road, but a muddy lane.

***

As soon as we arrive at the house, Al and I run out into the garden, across the stone patio, through the yellow grass, but then we stop. Our father is talking to the doctor. The doctor's white hair catches the light as he leans over the picnic table. My father flicks the ashes from his cigarette onto the grass.   Max is sleeping between them.   Al and I walk slowly across the grass holding hands.   When we stand a few feet away, my father glances up.

"How are my girls?" he asks, brushing his hand through his hair.

"Fine," I say and Al says a split second afterwards, "fine."

My father laughs.

I bend over and stroke Max's soft ears. His nose is dry. I wonder if he is sick.

"Do you want to see me do a handstand?" Al asks.

"Okay," father says.

She stands on her hands and the skirt of her dress falls over her face. We can see her underwear. It's white with little pink bows on the front.

"What about you?" Father asks. "Don't you want to do a handstand?"

"No," I say.

"Go on," he says.

"No," but then I stand on my hands and the skirt of my dress falls over my face and I'm glad because it's all dark and my father can't see me go red.   Through the material, I can just make out the outline of his legs and shoes. The blood rushes to my head. I try to focus on keeping my legs straight. I balance for a long time, until I hear aunt Ethel say, "What are you doing? You're much too big to do that." Then I jump down and pull on my dress, tugging on the skirt with both hands as if I could stretch it to cover my knees.

Ethel stands beside Mummy who is holding a blue jug my father bought on their honeymoon in Italy. Ethel's cheeks are almost purple. She walks over to the shade. I lie beside Al. We both rest our heads on Max's stomach. It's making funny noises like he's hungry.

"I'm afraid there's not much food," Mummy says. "Some tomatoes from the vegetable garden and some lettuce. I found a can of tuna. A baguette. Juliet's gone with Luis into town to buy food, but they won't be back for some time."

"It's so hot no one's hungry anyway," my father says. He crushes his cigarette in a saucer, then plays with his cigarette pack. He twirls it round and round between his fingers.

149

"I'll be right back," Mummy says. We watch her walk through the long yellow grass where giant poppies with centers like spiders have multiplied. The sunlight makes Mummy's hair look gold and her dress very black. She walks very straight. We watch her disappear into the house.

"Such a hot day," Ethel says, from the shade. Without knitting needles, her hands look strange resting on her lap. She's sitting in one of the blue chairs. The one next to her is empty. It makes me think of Granny. I picture her wearing her mauve hat, knitting very fast.

"Yes," the doctor says. "It is a hot day."

"I don't think I've ever experienced such a hot day," Ethel says.

"I would have thought you would be used to the heat," my father says.

"The heat in Johannesburg is different. It's dry, not humid like this," Ethel says, sitting up straight.

The sky hangs over us like a low ceiling, a perfect blue with not one scratch. It's so quiet the buzzing of wasps and bees seems loud. But you can hardly hear the river. It flickers in the distance.

Everything else droops—the roses, the bushes, even the ivy leaves on the house.

When Mummy walks out of the kitchen, carrying a silver tray, she's accompanied by a man who seems familiar. As they come closer, I realize that he's the tramp we saw coming out of our house the first day and then from our tree. "I've invited him to have lunch with us," Mummy says. "The poor man hasn't eaten in more than a week."

The tramp bends slightly at the waist. "Bonjour," he says. "Bonjour. Bonjour." He's wearing a blue shirt that's ripped at the armpits. His pants are black and made of wool. He holds a brown hat in his hands. He stares at us, but you can't tell where he's looking because of his glass eye. He walks over to the only free chair besides Ethel. She draws herself up and looks the other way.

"I'm so sorry," Mummy says. "Today we don't have as much food as we usually do."

She prepares a plate with salad and tuna and some baguette and brings it over to the tramp.

She sits down between my father and the doctor, but closer to the doctor. As she passes the bread to my father, her sleeve dips in the dressing and my father reaches out. "Thanks," she says, smiling first at my father, then at the doctor. I heard Mummy tell Ethel that the doctor is a very jealous man because of his ex-wife. She had lovers come to their house.

"Why the hell did you invite him?" Father whispers.

"I felt sorry for him," Mummy answers.

"You could have given him a piece of bread. You didn't need to invite him to lunch."

The doctor mops up his salad dressing with a piece of bread.

"Is this some kind of joke?" My father asks. "It looks like he's even wearing some of my clothes."

"Oh no," Mummy says, but then she laughs and says he is. "I promise you I didn't know."

Maybe Mum didn't just float Dad's hat down the river. I picture his pants and his pink, white, and blue shirts swirling in the water by the dam.

Max's stomach is making all sorts of gurgling noises. Al says she can feel his stomach vibrating.

When the doctor finishes what is on his plate, he walks over to the tramp. He stands talking to him. He asks the tramp what he used to do. The tramp says he used to be a successful businessman. He had a beautiful wife. Three beautiful children. Then one day, he was backing his car out of the garage when he ran over a little girl. After that, he lost everything. The tramp asks the doctor if he has cigarettes but the doctor doesn't smoke. My father walks over and gives him two.

"Thank you," the tramp says. "I'll be going now."

"If you need help," the doctor says. "You can always stop by the clinic."

"I like to be outside," the tramp says, then he spits right by Daddy's feet. We watch him cross the yellow lawn, disappear round the side of the house.

"What a relief," Ethel says. "Really, Claire, what on earth—"

"She has to apologize even to a tramp," Father says.

"Gabriel, don't you want some tomatoes?" Mummy asks.

"No, thank you." I think of Granny eating tomatoes up in the vegetable garden, the way she ate them so fast as if she knew she didn't have much time.

"What about you, Al?" Mummy says.

"No thank you."

"We're not hungry," I say.

My mother whispers something to my father.

"Come over here, girls," my father says. "I have a surprise for you."

"A good or a bad one?"

"Why a good surprise," my father says. He reaches into a pink bag with yellow and purple peonies that must belong to his lady. He holds out cameras for each of us. "They're Polaroids. All you have to do is push the button and the pictures come out right away."

He takes one and photographs me and Al. Then we wait. The paper is gray. Gradually, we can see our heads, the outline of our silhouettes. Everything is under water and then it's not.

I tell my mother and my father and the doctor that I want to take a picture of them. Mummy smiles and looks straight at the camera. Father looks down at his cigarette. The doctor at my mother. I try to focus the camera so that Dad and the doctor's heads are chopped off, but I can't without cutting off Mum's too. I take a photograph of Ethel but she gets annoyed because I took the photograph while she was picking her teeth.

Al and I walk around the garden taking photographs of everything: the stone house with its ivy leaves, the river and the wood bridges, the bank of silver willows, our treehouses, even the cross where we buried our rabbit, the monkey, and Al's blanket. Al wants to know if they would be all right if we dug them up or if they would have been eaten by worms. I tell her they would have been eaten up.

***

When we get back, everyone has disappeared except our father who lies on a yellow deck chair, his long feet sticking over the edge, his face covered with little red blotches and his mouth wide open, letting out a soft regular snore. His book, its leaves awkwardly bent, lies like a dead pigeon next to a tube of cream.

We tiptoe around him. Our shadows pass over him, but he does not wake.

We take pictures. I focus one picture on his white stomach. It has lots of hair. He even has hair sticking out of his ears like Luis.

Al and I sit by the pool with our legs dangling in the water. I stare at my reflection, seeing one long braid, my black dress broken into pieces by the water. Al and I look like twins.

When my father wakes, he dives into the pool. Al and I watch him swim laps.

"Don't you want to take a dip?" he asks. "It feels great."

Al and I look at each other, then we jump in hand in hand with our clothes on, even our shoes.

"What's this?" Daddy says. "It's becoming a bad habit."

"We like swimming in our clothes," I say.

But the water feels warm and oily and our clothes weigh us down. Soon we get out and stand in our wet clothes. I hope they're dry by the time Juliet gets back.

Father dries himself off and pulls on his clothes. He suggests we go for a walk. We walk along the bank of silver willows. He keeps stopping, though, and passing his hand through his hair, looking back at the house, as if he's changed his mind. I pull on his jacket sleeve and he turns and looks at me and says, "Yes?" and I say "Nothing."

"The doctor seems like a nice man," my father says.

"I guess," I say.

"He brushes his teeth every few hours," Al says.

"Does he?" Daddy laughs.

"And he doesn't like Max," Al says.

"Well, Max can be a nuisance," Daddy says.

"And he has to pee a lot," Al says.

"Boy, the things you girls find out," Daddy says. "I'd hate to hear what you say about me."

"We don't say anything about you," I say.

"Not one thing," Al says.

"I don't know if that's good or bad," my father says.

"It's good," I say, running ahead.

There are no shadows today. The sun is so bright the leaves of the trees seem as if they were made of metal.

"Come back," Daddy calls. "Why don't we skip?"

"It's too hot," I say.

"Come on."

"I'm too old."

He laughs. "Well, I'm not." He takes Al's hand and they skip through the grass. He stops halfway down the bank and gestures for me to catch up, but I won't. I'm too old to skip and jump. I'm going to be eleven in two months and eight days.

Al and my father are sitting on one of the wood bridges staring down at their reflections on the water. I sit next to Al.

"You both know that I'm not perfect," he says. "But your mother isn't either, you know."

"Nobody's perfect," I say.

"Yes, I know, but I think it's time you girls heard my side of the story. After all, there always are two sides to a story."

"I don't want to know," I say.

"Do you remember that ex-boyfriend of hers who came to visit us? Let's see, about a year ago?"

"What did he look like?" Al asks.

"He was tall and blond. You know, he was the man from Africa."

"The one she fell in love with when she was sixteen?" Al says.

"The one she fell out of love with because he shaved his beard," our father says.

I stare at my father. He has turned around and is now facing us. I notice three lines stretching across his forehead. The one at the top is the same length as the bottom one.

I focus on the sound of the water rushing; then I pretend I'm deaf.

"Yes," he says. "In our bedroom. I even lent him a pair of socks."

I try to imagine the bedroom with its pale yellow wallpaper and bright blue flower design, its gold carpet and my mother with the man from Africa wrapped in a white sheet, lions lurking behind the dark wood closet. But I can't really picture it. All I remember is the smell of bacon in the morning when the man from Africa appeared, and the little bracelets of black elephant hair he gave us.

***

I lean against Mummy the way I used to with Granny but she's talking with the doctor, so I join Al by the pool.

We lie on the smooth stones that surround the pool's edge. I rest my cheek on the stone. It's hot.

Ethel is nodding to sleep in her chair. From time to time, she wakes up with a start, just the way Tiger, the cat, wakes when she lies under a lamp and it suddenly gets too hot.

"Would you like some tea?" Mummy asks Ethel.

"Oh no," Ethel says. "Thank you."

"I wonder what could be taking Juliet and Luis so long," Mummy says. "It's just as well we didn't wait for them to eat."

"Yes," Ethel says. "I wonder—"

"Let's just hope they didn't stop in a cafe-bar," my father says. "I'll never forget the time I picked her up at the airport."

"Or maybe they got lost," our mother says. "You know what Luis is like."

"What did you say about the airport?" Ethel asks.

Mummy places one finger over her lips.

"I was just saying that you should allow for plenty of time," our father says.

"I'm not going to the airport," Ethel says.

"Oh that's right," Daddy says. "I'd forgotten about your fear of planes."

I put my hand in the water, but it's so warm it doesn't cool me. "You'll have to meet Françoise," our father says.

The doctor looks down at his cup. Mummy puts her hand on the doctor's forearm.

My father takes out a cigarette and offers one to the doctor, who says no thanks.

Then it's quiet and we can hear the wasps and the bees. There's no sign of Max. I wonder where he could be.

Mummy's hand moves from the doctor's forearm to his hand.

"I don't understand," Ethel says, suddenly, from the shade.

Nobody asks her what. Mummy walks over and puts her arm around Ethel, but she continues to look straight ahead as if she doesn't recognize Mummy. She allows Mummy to take her inside.

***

In the garage sunlight filters through cracks. The orange canoe gleams. We have scrubbed it and patched the hole. It's all ready. We're just waiting for the right time. We can't decide whether to leave in the day or the night. We've placed our belongings inside:

155

the jar with the brown beads, Mum's doll with no eyes, Daddy's cracked binoculars, Granny's bandage, the box that used to hold the dried fruit. We even found a black and white photograph that's missing just one corner of Granny and Ethel standing on the QEII; Granny is smiling and has one white gloved hand in the air and it looks like she's waving to us, saying toulalou.

We climb into the canoe and read our books. We're both reading *The Wolves of Whilloughby Chase*. But we each have our own copy. It's all about these girls who get left behind with their evil governess who puts them into an awful orphanage when their parents are reported dead, but then the girls escape and it turns out the parents are alive and the governess is punished.

I ignore the grownups calling for us. "Gabriel. Al. Come and say goodbye to your father." I stand up on a box and peer through the window streaked with mud. I can see the doctor and our father standing beside his green Porsche.

"Still no sign of Juliet and Luis," our father says.

"No," Mummy says. "Who knows when they will be back. But where are the children?"

"They're probably up in their treehouses," Daddy says. "Gabriel. Al."

I picture Daddy searching the garden, walking along the bank of silver willows, not finding us in our treehouses, checking the house, peering behind doors and inside closets. But he calls our names again then stares through the garage window. I stare right at him. I can make out his beaked nose and his wide forehead and his lips, but he can't see me because I'm in the dark. I imagine the glass shattering. I think I hear it cracking. I picture shards of glass on my father's shirt and in his hair. But then I recognize the sound of his Porsche, the vroom it always makes and I wander over to the other side of the garage, where muskrats used to hang. They're gone, but it feels as if they're still there. Al asks me to help her with the word predicament.

***

Around four, I hear a car drive across the gravel yard. Al and I rush to the window of our bedroom. We watch Juliet climb out of Luis's car. She's wearing her wig and her favorite black nylon dress with the gold chain.

156

"We were so worried," Mummy says as she comes out of the house. "What happened?"

"We had some car problems," Juliet says.

Luis says something in Spanish and waves his hand in the air. He looks very angry, then he says, "She make me wait and wait. I do not know what to do."

"Oh Juliet," Mummy says.

"I don't know what he's talking about," Juliet says. "I was waiting for him for hours and hours."

"Well," Mummy says. "I suppose there's no point in getting into an argument. Everyone is here safe and sound. Juliet, are you sure you're feeling all right?"

"Never felt better," Juliet says, as she stumbles into the house. Soon we hear her stomping upstairs. She stops outside our door, but doesn't come inside. She knocks something over, then curses. I lipsing her curses to Al.

Mummy just misses hearing them.

"Gabriel," she says. "Would you go and tell Ethel the car is ready? Be especially nice. Poor aunt, I don't know what she'll do without Granny."

I walk slowly down the stairs. I don't want to be the one to get Ethel. I wander through the living room where the curtains hang limply and roses droop over the rims of vases, their petals dropping onto the wood surfaces covered with pollen. I pass one hand over the coffee table and my palm comes away green. Even the flies circle listlessly. They fly into the glass panes, then lay stunned on the window sills before starting once again.

I stare at the portrait of the little girl whose head is too big for her body. But now, it's her eyes I notice, tiny mean brown eyes which seem to stare at me.

Ethel's not in Granny's room.

Granny's hat lies on top of one of the suitcases. I put it on my head and stand in front of the mirror. Over the summer my nose and forehead seem to have broadened. My eyes are the same color as Daddy's. I look like him. I wish I looked more like Mummy and Granny.

Ethel's sitting on her bed in her room, legs stretched in front of her, her hands resting on her knees. She seems to be staring at her feet, but as soon as she sees me, she straightens up. She stands and twists her skirt around her waist.

"I suppose it's time."

"Yes," I say.

"You be a good girl."

"Yes."

"I don't suppose I will see you for a very long time."

"Yes."

"Come here," she says.

I walk over to her. She presents her brow and I kiss it. She smells of peppermint, but of something else. Like Granny. I try to give her a hug, but she holds herself stiffly away. She's not used to hugs.

"Go and tell Luis to come for the suitcases," she says, turning away and bending over one of them. Her shirt has come undone in back and you can see the knobs of her spine. She sobs. I wonder whether to say something, but then I run out.

Mummy, Ethel, and I watch Luis load the suitcases into the trunk. The doctor helps him tie the last two suitcases on top of the car. Aunt Ethel climbs into the front seat. I watch her moving her mint round and round in her mouth, faster and faster. Luis pulls out a cap. It's blue with gold trim.

"Where did you get that?" Aunt Ethel asks.

"I bought it in Paris. A special shop."

"It looks perfectly ridiculous," she says.

"Oh Ethel," mother says.

"You're to take it off immediately," Ethel says.

Luis takes it off, but holds it in his hands as if reluctant to put it down again.

"If he wants to wear it——" Mummy says.

"I won't drive with him wearing that ridiculous cap," she says.

"I'm so sorry, Luis," mother says.

"It's all right. Miss Ethel upset today. I wear it tomorrow."

The doctor, mother, and Al and I laugh.

"I'll see you in a few weeks," mother says, leaning into the car.

The gold car starts up and we watch it slowly drive across the gravel yard, through the white gate and up the hill. It disappears over the top.

Ethel left me Granny's hat, but sitting on top of the chest of drawers in the shade it looks faded and old and hardly like hers. A corset hangs over a chair, the white elastics twisting in the breeze. I look through the drawers and shelves. They're empty, not a thing is left, but then I find, slipped beneath the pale blue paper lining of one of the drawers, a handkerchief with a trace of pink lipstick in its corner and I remember the way Granny used to curl her upper lip and rub her front teeth with her handkerchief.

***

It's Al's idea. We've always wanted to see what it's like but we've never dared to before. We're going under the house, beneath Granny's room, where there used to be a wheel for the mill. We're standing in the river. We're wearing boots, but the water is so high that water has got in them. I can feel stones and even snails under my feet. I can see to the other side of the house, but I don't feel like walking under. I'm afraid I'll lose my footing and get swept under. The ceiling has gray bugs and cobwebs. Al's not afraid. She smiles at me, then lets herself drop. She floats down. I call to her, but she doesn't hear me. She's swept all the way to the other side. I look up. Juliet's leaning out her window. She's looking straight at me, but she doesn't say anything. I duck under. The current is quite strong. I take a step, then another. Suddenly the floor dips and I lose my footing. I swallow water. I'm going to suffocate. I feel a muskrat brush my leg. I'm going to drown. I kick my legs and arms as hard as I can, then I let myself float. I drift out of the passage and the sun is warm and the red poppies so red it's hard to look at them.

Al is sitting on the grass, struggling to take off her boots. I climb out and walk up and down the bank, making a squelching noise with my boots. I keep expecting Juliet to step out of the house. I picture her running out with her hair standing on end, but she doesn't.

Twenty

The garden is filled with shadows. At this hour, five o'clock, the shadows are of the branches of the trees, not of the leaves or trunks. We're lying in the hammock with Mummy. We're covered with tiny specks of white from the dandelions we have been blowing. "He loves me. He loves me not. He loves me. He loves me not," Al says. I thought you could only play that game with the petals of flowers. But Mummy says you can play it with anything. Juliet can tell you the first letter of the name of the person you are going to marry with the peel of an orange. She peels the orange from the top with a knife and then goes round and round and whatever shape the peel comes out is the first letter of your future husband.

"Girls," Mummy says, taking our hands. "There's something I have to tell you."

I look up through the leaves at the sky. It's still blue, but the air is cooler. The evening is almost here.

"We know," I say.

"Xavier has asked me to marry him," Mummy says. She lifts our hands and the gold bracelets which used to belong to Granny jingle. They catch the sun throwing light onto the grass. Mummy lets her hands drop and hugs us both tightly. Her hair brushes my cheek and I remember how Daddy used to pull it over his head and say he wished she could give him some.

"What did you say?" I ask.

"I told him I wanted to talk to you girls first."

"Is Juliet going to stay with us?" Al asks.

"I haven't really thought about it. But yes, I expect so, at least at first. Certainly, she'll need to look after you while I'm away in South Africa."

"Are we going to have to change apartments?" I ask.

"We haven't decided yet. It might be more convenient to move into Xavier's apartment. On the other hand, it's a bit far from your school."

"Will we have to change schools?" Al asks.

"Would you like to?"

"No," I answer.

"Well, we'll see. This September, anyway, you'll be going back to your schools."

"How long will you be in S.A.?" I ask.

"It all depends on how much Ethel needs me. It's such a shame she refuses to fly. We would have been over there by now. She should be getting on board the QEII in an hour or so."

In the distance we can hear the hunters. They have someone beat the fields so that the pheasants will fly up and then they shoot them. Granny used to say the poor birds don't have much of a chance.

"Did I tell you about the time Granny brought us to America?" Mummy says.

"No," I say, though she has told us many times.

"We kept reading our books and poor Granny kept saying, but look outside, look at those trees. Look at that landscape."

As if he had been waiting for Mummy to tell us, the doctor appears from around the house. He walks with quick tiny steps across the lawn over to the hammock. He helps Mummy down. We watch them kiss on the mouth. He holds her very tight as if he's afraid she'll disappear. He takes her hand and Mum takes Al's and he reaches out to take mine, but I run ahead. I run and run through the grass until I reach the house. I climb up onto the window sill beneath Juliet's bedroom and I hoist myself up so that I'm peering into her bedroom. She's fast asleep on the floor again. She's holding her calendar rolled up in one hand as if she had been trying to swat a fly or a wasp before falling asleep.

When I peer through the living room window, Mummy and the doctor are sitting on the couch. Al is by their feet, with her head resting on Max. "We'll have to have the grass mowed," the doctor says, "before we put the house on the market."

"Yes," Mummy says. "I haven't told the children yet."

"There's no rush. It won't happen for a few months yet."

"You know I don't really care," Mummy says.

"I don't think I could live with someone whose main concern was interior decorating."

I tiptoe into the living room and lie beside Al and rest my head on Max. I lipsing to Al that the house is going to be sold. We're going to be orphans. They're going to send us to live in one of the public housing apartment buildings and we'll have nothing to eat, except for water and bread.

Twenty-One

Al and I are trying to roll up the carpet, but Max keeps sitting on it so we have to stop and shoo him away. There are boxes everywhere. All the boxes are numbered. The number one boxes are going across the street to the doctor's house. The number two boxes are going to our apartment in Paris. The doctor is going to move in with us. The number three boxes are going to Daddy's apartment. We keep forgetting to mark them so we have to open them to figure out where they belong. All the slipcovers and curtains have been sent to the dry cleaners. The house looks naked, like an old lady. In place of the paintings, there are white squares or rectangles. The only painting nobody wanted is of the little girl whose head is too big for her body. It's standing in one corner of the living room.

Juliet's seated in the blue and white chair. She has her legs stretched before her. Her feet are bare and she reaches down and massages her bunions. Al calls them onions. It's a good name.

"I think I'm going to have the operation after all," she says.

"What operation?" Al asks.

"To have my bunions removed."

"It must be so painful," I say. "I don't think I would if I were you."

"The problem is that you have to be able to put up your feet for at least a few weeks. Now, when am I going to be able to do that?"

"Well, I'm sure you could take a few weeks off, Juliet," Mummy says, as she passes through the living room, carrying a big box filled with Granny's romance novels.

"What are you doing with those?" I ask.

"Well," Mummy says. "I was thinking of giving them away."

"Oh no, you can't."

"But you've read all of them."

"I want to read them again. Besides, they're in English. No one will want them anyway."

"All right," Mummy says, passing the box over to me.

"I suppose I should be getting up," Juliet says. "They're still those drawers in the kitchen."

"Please, Juliet," Mummy says. "If you're not feeling up to it, do take a rest. You can even have the day off if you want."

"No, no," Juliet says. She gets up slowly. We watch her walk through the living room, one hand pressed to her lower back. She wanders into the entrance hall. Soon we hear a terrific clatter of dishes, the sound of glass broken.

"Oh dear," Mummy says. "I wish she wouldn't help. She's usually so efficient, but our packing seems to have upset her."

"It's not just that," I say.

"What is it?" Mummy says.

"Nothing," I say.

"She says she's not wanted," Al says.

"Oh dear. The problem is that Xavier and I have been talking about whether or not we should keep her so I don't want to say anything too misleading—"

More pots and pans are slammed in the kitchen. A door is closed. Mummy says she's going upstairs to finish the attic.

Al and I stare through the glass door at the grass which has grown so tall, it no longer looks like a lawn. It reminds me of a forest. Wild flowers and thistles have grown and the grass is yellow and coarse and I can no longer run my fingers through the blades. Even the path Daddy mowed has grown, but it still hasn't caught up with the rest and looks strange stopping halfway.

We have to be careful walking across the lawn now because snakes can easily hide in the tall grass. Soon the lawn will look like the wild field at the end of the garden. The doctor tried to mow it, but he almost fell into the river. He's gone back to Paris until Mum returns from South Africa.

Then we hear Mummy call. "Gabriel, Al. Come and tell me if you still want these." We walk slowly through the living room up the back stairs, through our room to the attic. Mummy holds up two enormous baby dolls: one has white hair, the other yellow hair. Their white lacy dresses have mold. "Yes," we say. We take the dolls outside and place them inside the wheelbarrow and then we wheel it across the lawn as fast as we can and tip the dolls into the water. At first they float. The one with the gold hair flips onto her face, while the other one looks up at the sky; then they get caught in weeds. We watch them slowly fill with water and sink. Al wants to know if the fish will eat them. I say, yes.

Twenty-Two

"I wish I didn't have to go," Mummy says, leaning out the window of her gray Alpha Romeo, "and leave you girls."

I stare down at my shoes. The trees and the sky are reflected in the black patent leather. I touch Granny's pearls around my neck. I keep running my fingers over them, again and again.

"Why can't we go with you?" Al asks, jumping up.

"Darling, it's not going to be much fun, and what would you do while I was helping Ethel? To tell you the truth, I'm rather dreading it. But I'll be back very soon, and I'll call every day."

"I'll take good care of them," Juliet says. She's not wearing make-up today and her face looks unusually pale, as if she has no eyelashes.

"Fart face," I lipsing to Al.

"Fart face," she lipsings.

Mummy starts up the car, but it makes a funny noise and the engine dies and I think she won't be able to leave. She tries it again and still she can't start it up. I don't want to hope but I can't help hoping. She tries it once more, the engine runs, and we watch the car slowly cross the gravel, roll through the white gate and up the hill. It feels as if I'm sinking deeper and deeper into water, as if my feet will never touch the floor.

I keep expecting the car to reappear at the top of the hill. I can't believe she's really gone. I run and run up the hill. I don't listen to Juliet calling. When I reach the top, I stare down the long white road that cuts through the yellow fields. I expect the car to reappear after the dip, but it doesn't. There isn't even a cloud of dust and the thickets are still.

"What shall we do now?" Juliet asks, when I get down to the house. She places one hand on Al's shoulder and the other on mine. Her hand is broad and heavy, so different from Mummy's.

"Nothing," I answer and twist away. I duck under her arm and step into the house. The entrance hall is cool and dark. Mummy's perfume still lingers in the air. The whitewashed wall is reflected in the mirror. For a second, I don't recognize myself. My legs and arms are too long, my feet too big. My father's prediction has come true. I think I can see a dip in my nose. I screw my face up into the ugliest expression.

"Very attractive," Juliet says, standing beside me. "Let's see if I can do a better one." She twists her mouth to one side, closes one eye, then presses her finger to the tip of her nose. "We're going to have a fabulous day." She teases her hair with the tips of her fingers.

"What about me?" Al asks. "Look at me."

"You look like a hamster," Juliet says.

I slip away. The house is so empty it feels as if the walls are made of paper and not of stone, as if the slightest breeze will make it fly up into the air. In the living room the blue velvet curtains have been removed. There's no carpet, just the white-and-black tiled floor. Dust covers the furniture. I stroke the top of the mahogany chest, then sit down on the sofa and stare at the empty space above the mantelpiece where the painting used to be with the little girl with the grown-up face.

Juliet stands in the doorway with one hand pressed to her lower back. Al sits next to me.

"I just need a bit of a lie-down, girls," Juliet says. "And then we'll do something really fun. Entertain yourselves, but don't get into trouble."

We watch her walk across the living room. I listen to her slow heavy footsteps up the back stairs. Her door closes with a bang. We continue to sit for a few minutes; then it's so quiet I jump up and run from room to room. We stop in Ethel's room and stare through the glass door at the weeping willow. It bends so low that the tips of its branches touch the grass like an old lady with long hair leaning over to tie her shoe. Al stands on Ethel's bed and jumps up and down, making the bed creak and then the two of us jump, holding hands to keep our balance. We jump and jump. I jump higher and higher. I don't care if I fall. I hear the springs creaking. We can feel them beneath our bare feet. We laugh at the thought of what Ethel would say if she could see us. We laugh and laugh until tears stream down our faces and I can't tell if Al is laughing or crying.

I tell Al not to worry. If Mum doesn't come back, we'll run

away and find her. I asked Mum to give me her address so that I could write to her, but really I wanted it in case she doesn't come back. She packed all her clothes and all her toiletries. She even took the orange dress she never wears.

We climb up to the attic to play our favorite game one last time. We walk across the beam, placing one foot in front of the other, toes touching heel, our arms outstretched, our shadows slanting the same way. We imagine that there are not two of us, but four. We give names to the others, our shadows, our names backwards, hers is Xela mine is Lierbag. Then we try to stand so close together we have only one shadow, and we manage to but it's a strange-looking one, wide and different from either mine or hers, bulky, like an old lady carrying many bags. We hold each other very tight, then we make the game more difficult by trying to hop across the beam, first on one foot, then the other and then we see who can run across it faster. We play for a long time, then we stare at the drawings of sailboats. They're done in red ink and cover one whole wall. We wonder who drew them and wish we had a sailboat instead of a canoe. Tonight we're going down the river.

When we return to Juliet's room, she's not in her bed. There are bottles lying on the floor. One is overturned. "Juliet has peepeed," Al says. Puzzle pieces are strewn across the floor. Her clothes are piled in one corner, her books stacked in another. One whole section of the green cloth covering the wall has come undone and hangs like a sail. We cannot find her suitcase.

For a moment, we think she's gone, but then we hear water coming from the other side of the house. Juliet's in Mummy's bathroom. I hear her singing, "All I want is a room somewhere far away from the cold night air," her favorite song from her favorite movie, *My Fair Lady*. She's seen it six times. I pretended to have a stomachache the last time she wanted to go because she always embarrasses me by singing out loud all the songs. She says she likes the movie even though Julie Andrews should have played the part. I knock on the bathroom door. "We're hungry."

"I'll only be a minute," she says.

I knock again. "We're hungry."

"We're hungry. We're hungry." Al and I shout, banging on the door louder and louder.

I don't like Juliet using Mummy's bathroom, but I don't say

anything when she comes out with her hair wrapped in a towel like a turban. I expect her to scold us, but she doesn't say anything. She's wearing a red terry cloth robe that looks like one my father owned. Her cheeks are flushed, and she doesn't look tired anymore. "Follow me," she says and claps her hands in the air as if she held a tambourine. "We're going to have a fabulous time together. We'll have a feast. There's brie, boursin, Saint Andre. Three baguettes. Some left over hashi parmentier. You like that, don't you? What else? I've got wine, champagne, sponge cake. No more dieting for me. I'm tired of dieting and anyway I only get fatter. Perhaps if I eat more, I'll lose weight." We follow her downstairs, through the living room and up our stairs. She leaves wet footsteps on the wood floor. All the time she continues to sing, "All I want is a room somewhere." She steps between the bottles and books in her room as if they weren't there. She sorts through her dresses. "Al, go get my make-up case. Gabriel, Kleenexes. I think there're some in your mother's bathroom."

When I return, Juliet is pulling on her pantyhose, threading her way between bottles and books and papers. Slowly, she lifts one leg, then the other. She goes round the bedroom, passing open windows. She seems to be dancing to an imaginary tune, but this time it's a slow sad melody. It's late afternoon and the sun casts a pink shadow across one wall and streaks the green cloth gold.

At last she stops and pulls on her dress, a new dress that has gold buttons that are so heavy they droop.

"Are they wasps or bumble bees?" I ask.

"What?"

"The buttons," I say.

"I think they're birds," she says, and I imagine them flying off one by one. She stands sideways in front of our mirror and pulls in her stomach. She tightens the black belt by one notch.

I remember Al saying, "Are you going on a secret-rendezvous?" at the beginning of the summer.

Juliet applies her lipstick and puts some above her lips so they look gigantic.

"Here're the tissues," I say.

She presses her brow with them, then slips them into her bodice.

"Now, you need to get into something else," she says.

"Oh no," we say.

"How can we celebrate if we are not dressed for a celebration?" She asks.

"We don't want to have a celebration."

Al and I don't change into our dresses, but when we come into the kitchen, Juliet doesn't say anything. The smell of meat and potatoes fills the room. The windows are covered with mist. The ceiling with its wood beams seems very low. The kitchen feels smaller than at the beginning of the summer.

"We'll have dinner here," Juliet says. "It's so much cheerier."

"All right," we say.

"You can lay the table, Al. Gabriel, why don't you mix the dressing for the salad? I'm heating up the hashi parmentier."

She uncorks a bottle of red wine and fills her glass to the brim.

"We're going to have a celebration," she says, again.

But it doesn't feel like a celebration. We're just having the leftovers from yesterday.

Max keeps passing wind under the white table.

"I thought we would start with a little of that potato and leek soup your mother made the other day," she says, ladling it out.

We sit down to eat at the round white table. We have to be careful not to lean on it because it wobbles. I don't slurp my soup, but I deliberately place my spoon so that it's not parallel to my mouth, but perpendicular. I wait for Juliet to notice. She stares at me, but says nothing.

"Tell us about the Second World War," I say as I always do.

"Well, you know, I used to work as a nurse during the war," she says, putting her glass of wine down on the table.

"Was it better than being a nanny?" I ask.

"In some respects, but one of the advantages of being a nanny is that you get to live in different places." Juliet lived in Lebanon, where it rains sometimes on one side of the street and on the other it's sunny. She had the best of times in Lebanon because there were so many nannies there. They used to meet for afternoon tea. Al and I lipsing "But one of the advantages..." We know it all by heart.

"Being a nurse is very hard work and there were things that weren't so pleasant, like changing bed pans." She cuts herself a piece of brie and balances it delicately on a chunk of bread. She whispers, "I even had to wash men's private parts."

We stop eating and stare at Juliet. We can't believe it. She's never told us that before. She's never used the words "private parts" in front of us. She drinks more wine, sticking her tongue out as she does. Her tongue has creases. Two creases down the middle. I lipsing to Al, "Does my tongue have creases?" I stick out my tongue and she says, "no." She wants to know if she has creases.

"What are you two doing sticking your tongues out?" Juliet asks. "You look like dogs."

"We're hot," I say sticking out my tongue again, making a panting noise.

Juliet sticks hers out again. We're all three sticking our tongues out and making panting noises. Al and I look at each other. We can't believe that Juliet is being so silly. We've never seen her like this before.

She changes the soup bowls for plates with hashi parmentier and spinach. The hashi parmentier is almost all meat. She puts a bit of it on her fork, then some spinach. She always says it's good to mix everything, but I like to keep everything separate. I slowly put my hands on the table and Al imitates me, but Juliet still doesn't say anything. Then I say, "Max has passed wind."

Juliet carefully places her fork and knife together on her plate and I expect her arm to whip out, but she just laughs and says, "Max has passed wind."

"I've passed wind too," Al says.

"Me too," I say.

"It must be the meat in the hashi parmentier," Juliet says.

"I farted," I say.

"I did too," Al says.

"Now, you know you're not supposed to say that," Juliet says. "That word is just too vulgar." She takes another sip from her wine, sticking her pinky out.

Al and I imitate her and I think for sure she'll get mad, but she laughs. Her laugh is very deep and sounds just like a man's. But I don't feel like laughing.

Juliet says we don't have to do the cleaning. We can do it tomorrow. She's never said that before either. "Let's have dessert in the living room," she says. She tells me to carry the sponge cake, while Al takes the champagne. We place them carefully on the coffee table. Juliet kicks off her shoes and tiptoes round the room with her hands on her hips. She sings, " The rain in Spain stays mainly in the plain." We stand and watch Juliet dance, and she tells us to come. I tell Al to stay with me, but Al puts her hands on Juliet's hips. "The rain in Spain stays mainly in the plain," they sing. They dance round and round the living room while I sit on the couch and cut lines across the top of the sponge cake.

Juliet stops and says, "How about a game of cards?"

"I don't feel like it," I say.

"Oh come on."

"No," I say.

Juliet unrolls the carpet and sits down cross-legged. Her dress slips up her knees and I can see her underwear. Al sits opposite her. They play gin rummy and Juliet keeps winning. "What luck," she cries. "Lucky in cards, unlucky with men, that's me." She finishes the bottle of red wine and starts on the champagne. She says she's very thirsty. We ask her if we can have a sip and she says, "but just a sip." I think it's awful. It's so bitter.

It's still light outside, but the air is cooler and the sky turning from pink to mauve.

"Are you sleepy?" I ask Al.

"No," she says, but her eyes keep closing.

"Don't we have to go to bed?" I ask.

"Oh no," Juliet says. "It's still much too early. I tell you what. Why don't I do a belly dance?"

"Okay," we say, but I don't really feel like it.

She pulls off her dress, stands in her black underwear and bra, stretches her arms out, and curls her fingers. She moves only the bottom part of her body. She keeps the top completely still. She moves her hips from side to side. Her face remains serious and she stares ahead. I stare at her belly button and wish she would stop. I wish Mummy were here.

Juliet lets herself drop onto the floor. She pours more champagne in her glass and it overflows onto the carpet.

Then, I don't know why, I say, "Juliet, you're drunk."

"No, I'm not," Juliet says. "Don't you dare say that." Her arm swings out and she hits my head from behind.

"Don't you hit me."

"I'll do whatever damn well pleases me," she says.

"It's not fair," I say. I jump up and run out the living room door into the garden. I run and run and run across the wood bridges, along the bank of silver willows. I hear footsteps behind me. It's Al. We climb up into my treehouse and sit side by side on the bunk bed of logs. Now and then, one of the pots hanging from a branch clanks. We've got a carpet at our feet, and above us, hanging from a branch, the painting of the girl with the grownup face.

"She hit me too," Al says. "But I didn't say anything."

"Pig."

"Fart face."

"Bunion lady."

"Onion lady."

The sky is mauve like Granny's hat and the trees are black. The grass looks blue. I hear a lark, then the plash of a muskrat. We watch the sky gradually darken, but it's still light. The sky is purple. We're all alone. Just the two of us.

We'll never go back.

Then we hear Max barking. We see Juliet come out of the house. She wanders along the opposite bank calling, "Gabriel, Al," but we don't answer. She lies down in the grass and I think I can hear her crying, but we continue to hide.

"Are you crying?" Al asks.

I shake my head. She places her arm around me. I can feel her sticky fingers on my neck.

"Cheer up," she says, in her pretend-grownup voice. "Things will get better."

"No, they won't," I say, staring at the river. I think I can see our faces beneath the water, peering up at us. But then they vanish and I stare at the reflection of the trees which stretch all the way to the other bank. Gradually, the sky darkens. The birds are quiet, the garden hushed and still. I can no longer make out Juliet lying on the grass. I imagine her sitting asleep in her bed with her head pressed against the wall.

"Let's go back," Al says and I agree, but then Al says she wants her blanket, the white one with the blue flowers we buried. We search and search but we can't find the cross we planted among the ivy leaves. Al cries and cries. Something brushes my ankle and I cry out, imagining it's a muskrat. "Let's go," I tell Al and we run all the way to the house.

Max comes bounding out. He barks loudly, stands on his back paws, and rests his front paws on my chest. His nails dig into me, but I don't mind.

The lattice door closes behind us with a bang and the glass tinkles, but then it's quiet. All I can hear is the river running beneath the house. I listen so hard I think I can hear Granny and Daddy and Mummy's voices in the sound of rushing water. I picture the water running beneath the house. I wonder what it would be like to be sucked under. Al's hearing aid squeaks. She takes my hand. Our footsteps echo as we tiptoe into the living room. It's completely dark except for the moonlight filtering through the windows. At first, all I can make out is the outline of the furniture: the top of the couch, the mantelpiece, the lamp overturned on the carpet. Then I notice the flies eating the sponge cake left on the coffee table. They buzz around the half-empty champagne glass. Juliet's shoes look strange lying in one corner.

"Juliet," I shout.

"Juliet," Al shouts, but there's only silence. We walk up the stairs, holding onto the red velvet cord. We stand on the dark landing for a moment before pushing open her door. I expect to see her sitting in bed, but she's not there. I check underneath her bed to see if she's taken the box with the photographs of the children she looked after. It's still there, in one corner, with her bikini. We stand at her window and stare at the weeping willow lit by the moon.

We don't put on the lights. I want to pretend that it's just as it was before, at the beginning of the summer. There are no boxes. Light streams through the windows. Vases are filled with flowers. Granny's four pink suitcases stand in one corner of her room. I think I can hear Granny and Ethel whispering, "one pearl, one plain." I picture Granny sitting on the sofa holding her hat by the brim, stroking it absentmindedly as if it were a cat. Juliet dancing round the room. Mum and Dad sitting on yellow and white striped chairs, the skirt of my mother's white dress blowing up in the wind, her high pitched laugh drifting across the lawn as she tries to hold it down. "Let it go. Let it fly," I hear my father say.

We wander back down the stairs, through the living room and

into Granny's room with Max following us. I can hear the click, click, of his nails upon the floor. It's the only noise apart from the sound of the river.

We kneel on the water lily couch. We press our foreheads to the glass pane. We try to see the river, but it's so dark all I can see are slivers of silver. Ivy has grown across the window so that we can't open it anymore. In the moon, I think I can see Granny's face reflected, but a cloud passes in front of the moon and she disappears and we're alone again. The sky seems too big, the stars like the tiny beads Granny and Ethel used to knit.

Now and then the lights of cars beam through the living room, through the French doors into Granny's room. I watch the lights as they pass along the white wall and the book shelf. I know not to wait for the sound of tires crunching gravel. I know Daddy won't come back. Mummy is far away. Juliet is drunk and Granny lies beneath the earth.

I'm the only one who can look after Al.

"Don't worry, Al," I say. "Mummy says I'm very mature for my age."

"What's mature?" she asks.

"Grown up," I say.

"I'm a grownup too," she says, and I don't say anything though I know it's not true.

We sit for a moment longer, watching the garden turn from silver to black to silver when light falls upon our canoe. "Come," I say. "Let's go down the river."

"Okay," she says.

We tiptoe out the back door.

We walk along the white fence. The scent of the roses is very strong. We pluck the heads of the roses and fill the skirts of our dresses, letting the petals drop into the canoe.

We have to coax Max into the canoe by giving him a piece of baguette. The canoe tips from side to side as he gets in. It almost flips over. I check for our precious things: Daddy's broken binoculars, Granny's bandage, Mummy's doll, our Polaroid cameras, the box that used to hold the dried fruit, the wax paper still sprinkled with sugar. We lie on either side of Max. I like the smell of his hair and breath. I wonder if he misses his tail, the part that was chopped off, or if he has forgotten it.

We float down the silvery river. The fir trees are like dark shadows. One birch stands out, white, mysterious, alone. A water lily appears, then disappears. The moonlight spots the river. I think I hear Mummy's piano but then it's quiet. All I can hear is the water lapping the sides of our boat. The house grows smaller and smaller and it seems to me that the house is floating across the grass and not us floating down the river. The house seems to lift off and slowly glide toward us. Around a bend, it disappears. But we continue to drift down the river and beyond, towards a place we have yet to discover.